Wakefield P

murder at
the fortnight

Steve J. Spears has been a professional writer for thirty years. He is best known as the author of one of Australia's classic plays, *The Elocution of Benjamin Franklin*. He has published stage plays, children's books and a collection of his essays, *In Search of the Bodgie*.

Murder at the Fortnight is the first in his forthcoming thirteen-part series of darkly comic whodunit novels under the collective title of *The Pentangeli Papers*. *Murder by Manuscript* and *A Murder of Innocents* are due to follow soon.

Steve J. Spears lives a semi-hermit existence on a beach on the central coast of New South Wales and loves it.

34139 00107385 3

MURDER *at the* FORTNIGHT

STEVE J. SPEARS

Wakefield
Press

Wakefield Press
1 The Parade West
Kent Town
South Australia 5067
www.wakefieldpress.com.au

First published 2003

Copyright © Steve J. Spears, 2003

All rights reserved. This book is copyright. Apart from any fair dealing for
the purposes of private study, research, criticism or review, as permitted
under the Copyright Act, no part may be reproduced without written
permission. Enquiries should be addressed to the publisher.

Cover illustration by Katharine Stafford
Cover designed by Dean Lahn
Text designed and typeset by Clinton Ellicott
Printed and bound by Hyde Park Press

National Library of Australia
Cataloguing-in-publication entry

Spears, Steve J., 1951– .
Murder at the fortnight.

ISBN 1 86254 616 9.

1. Murder – Fiction. I. Title. (Series: Spears, Steve J., 1951 –
Pentangeli papers; v. 1).

A823.3

Publication of this book was assisted by the
Commonwealth Government through the
Australia Council, its arts funding and advisory body.

for Joanna Lumley

'There's no bizness like showbizness.'
Berlin

'Zounds! he dies: I had forgot the reward.'
Shakespeare

contents

prologue

It all really started five years ago when they let Robbie George out of prison. The sun was coming up, the tiny side gates opened and there he was. He looked great, like he'd been doing push-ups or jogging or whatever they do in stir for exercise. The officers made the usual jokes about how they hoped he'd enjoyed his stay and that he should come back soon, he he. Robbie laughed along with them and said at least he was leaving. The officers were still there, ho ho. And the obscenity of life in a lockup was papered over.

Apart from a few binges on potato vodka or vanilla extract, he'd been sober for six years and four months worth of lockup days and lockdown nights. Booze had gotten him there in the first place – gotten him drunk enough to steal a shotgun, stagger into a bank and say: 'This is a hold-up!'

At which point he tripped, fired at the ceiling and passed out from shock on the carpet. His arrest had been as smooth as the judge's face when she sent him down for twelve years.

One day in the yard – so goes the legend – he'd found a book of plays abandoned on the ground. Bored, he flipped through it, then read another, then went to the library, found books about plays, books about playwrights. Fearless, he picked up a biro and wrote the first of his four now world-famous prison plays, *Bar Code Blues*. It was the story of Sid and Johnny. Sid was about to be moved to another prison and Johnny was his cellmate girlfriend. They decide to get married. The play deals with one night – 12 hours until they take Sid away.

That might have been that except, during a Theatre In Prison workshop, a do-gooding left-wing actress – Cordelia Heath, who considered every inmate a political/economic prisoner – read the play and loved it.

Cordelia was a striking woman – tall, lithe, capable. Later, showbiz wits idly and lasciviously pondered how Robbie George must have felt when she'd come into his life bearing freedom, fame, money and adoration. Yum. Her off-blonde hair was, as usual, severely pulled back off her face, ending in an incongruously girlish ponytail. She almost always wore black baggy clothes as though ashamed of her notoriously fine body.

'I want to help you' were the first words she said to Robbie.

'How? Why?'

'I'll mount a production of *Bar Code* here. Because you're a very gifted writer.'

Bar Code Blues first saw the light of history in the ratty ancient prison library with a handful of cons acting the parts of cons. Cordelia had done her PR job well, blitzing the press with 'come see's' and nagging showbiz contacts with 'come show support's', and *Bar Code Blues* attracted an audience of civilians who that night saw a miracle. A thunderstorm. *Blues* was funny and true and it broke your heart. The season was extended to a week. Then three.

'Robbie,' said Cordelia during the first run, 'you don't have a great deal of modesty, do you?'

'Nope.' From the time he picked up the biro to the last

round of rapturous applause, Robbie had known that he'd created a masterpiece. He'd found a gift inside himself and delighted in it like a child delights in waves at the shore.

Cordelia got busy again, as only she could, on getting him released. She sold *Bar Code* to the State Theatre Company, which opened it to full houses in the Little Theatre before transferring it to a commercial management, where it ran over a year. Meanwhile Robbie, taking dictation from God, churned out three more plays. Cordelia hustled hardcore theatre lovers, then famous TV stars, then politicians to come gape at the Corrections Department's very own Genet. See him write! See how good! Increasing numbers of fans petitioned and demonstrated for Robbie's early release.

'After all, what more could a government want in terms of the rehabilitative power of . . .'

'Prison system that's the envy of the world.'

'Humanitarian gesture which . . .'

'Genius who . . .'

'The compassionate face of . . .'

So, after six years and four months, on a cold February day, they let Robbie George out. He was met by faithful fond Cordelia and a crowd of well-wishers and devotees dressed in their humanitarian best. Cordelia kissed him and whispered in his ear, then he was gone.

*

The second of Robbie's plays to be produced by the State Theatre Company was *Stone Garden*, a one-hander about an old lag who had worked for 30 years as the prison's stonemason-cum-gravedigger and finds out he's dying. It was even better than *Bar Code Blues* and its reception was amazing. Off-Broadway bought it and it sold out there. His last two prison plays, *Hangman* and *Where Have All The Flowers Gone?*, were

3

suddenly hot property and Cordelia Heath showed she knew how to play the capitalists at their own game. Not only had she become Robbie's lover, but she turned out to be a manager and negotiator of gusto and skill. The world was theirs.

As so often in showbiz – as so often in life – Robbie and Cordelia's moment in the sun was quickly rained out. For, after his release from prison, with his absolute freedom to write where and when he wanted, to enter or leave any room he chose, to select his own food and clothes and barber and TV shows, Robbie found himself paralysed.

'Lock me up, babe.'

'Lock you *up*?'

'Lock me up. If I'm not locked up, I can't write.'

So Cordelia locked him in a small closet for 14 hours at a stretch. He got her to don a screw's cap, scream abuse at him and slap him. She loved him. She believed in him. If he needs a warder as well as a lover, okay.

'Hard. Harder.'

WHACK! WHACK!

'Yell at me!'

WHACK!

'Pig! Dog!'

But nothing. Once the words had rained down on Robbie – golden coins to be spent or squandered. Now he knew that those four plays were all he had in him. He didn't know why or where, but he knew the gift had gone. So, a year to the day after his release, he got up from his writing desk, went to his long-ago pub, The Dog and Pony, and picked up where he'd left off.

Again and again, Cordelia carried him home and dried him out. Then one night – out of his mind – he lashed out at her with both fists, broke her nose, fractured her rib. Next morning, she threw him out. Refused to have him back.

Robbie moved into a room at The Dog and Pony, where all his money flowed out to drinking buddies and drinking buddies' buddies. The coins fell out of his raggedy suit as he fell into gutters – his pockets picked while he slept. He didn't care. He grieved over the nose and the rib and the broken love of the only woman who'd ever believed in him.

Sooner than seemed possible, he owed nineteen thousand dollars in gambling debts which he couldn't repay. A large crim came to visit Robbie in his drunken room. 'You owe Doc Mortaferi nineteen grand.'

Doc Mortaferi was the city's undisputed Mr Big, a self-made man who'd climbed to the top over the guilty bones of lesser crims.

'It's gone. The money's all gone,' said Robbie tonelessly.

So the large crim cut off Robbie's pinkie finger with garden shears.

Robbie George. Oh Lord, was it any wonder he was a showbiz legend?

part 1
killer love

How does it feel?
This killer love?
Not too heavy?
This killer love?
© *Angela Drumm*

1.

killer love

Stella Pentangeli was there when Reg Maundy was murdered most foully onstage during the thirtieth anniversary
production of *The Rocky Horror Show*.

It was pure luck Stella was at the show. She had developed
what she'd self-diagnosed as a serious phobia about large
numbers of people in dark places – that is to say, 'audiences' –
even though she'd loved the biz from the time she could toddle.
When she was six years old, she'd seen *Puss In Boots*, fallen in
love with this magical thing, and from then on her every con-
scious thought had been: I want to be a famous actress. She took
elocution lessons, dance lessons, acting lessons, you name it.

'Miss Pentangeli, you have no discernable acting talent.'
She was 17 and this was the verdict of the last of many patient
acting coaches. It was a bitter pill but Stella swallowed it
after a few weeks of ready-to-die teen heartache. If she couldn't
act in the biz, she'd shape it. She'd be a critic – a Pauline Kael,
a Kenneth Tynan – and serve Lady Showbiz that way.

Stella was as good as her word. She was the youngest journalist
ever to have an art critic's by-line in the national press. A
couple of years later she got her own weekly arts and showbiz
program on Channel 3 and proved perfect for the box. *S for*

Showbiz! S4S! quickly became a hit and she a household name. She was witty and attractive in a dark, neurotic way – grey eyes, impeccable diction, dark hair, an unfashionably full (and much lusted after) figure. She had been faithful to the biz and the biz had been faithful back. But, in the words of the poet, 'Golden lads and girls all must/as chimneysweepers come to dust'. Or, in Stella's case, come to their thirties. When she did, it started coming apart. Her not-particularly-loved parents were killed in a car crash and, weirdly, her hair turned snow white overnight. Her superiors at Channel 3 took her aside.

'Dye it,' they said. 'You look old.'

'No,' she said. 'It's a sign from my crappy parents. From beyond the grave.'

'Dye it.'

'I like it.'

The suits insisted. Sir Rex Clap, the legendary owner of Channel 3, took her into his wood and steel office. 'Dye it or fuck off,' he said in a voice coated with gravel.

'No.'

'Then fuck off.'

'Then fuck you.'

That was Stella's TV career. In a nano-second she was replaced by Cookie Creeme, a stupid 22-year-old blonde with tits and teeth. Stella was officially in breach of contract and – Oh lucky Channel 3! – she'd handed them her head and her career on a platter for a dollar.

For a season, like the prodigal son, Stella suffered for her sins, surviving on offal, eating with the pigs. She sank as low as ghostwriting for the stars. *My Crowded Life: The World of Max 'Mr Showbiz' Newton* by Max Newton or *Ouch!: Confessions of a Ballet Master* by Grigoria Olov, as told to Stella Pentangeli. Two thousand word articles like 'The Film Director: Auteur d'hauteur', 'Was Tennessee Williams *really* gay?', 'Are Russian

Gymnasts Pornographic?' Her life was in free-fall. Stella had run out of options. She and her beloved showbiz were done. In despair, she founded *The Pentangeli Papers* – a fortnightly online zine reviewing film/theatre/dance/TV etc.

*

The Rocky fucking Horror Show. Of all the shows for Stella, 36 year old near-has-been, to face her audience phobia and showbiz disdain, it had to be this turkey. As a teen she'd loved the movie and saw herself as Magenta the vamp, or Frank, or even little Columbia (but never Janet, of course). Seeing it now, Stella hadn't had sex in 17 (seventeen!) months and felt exactly like hapless helpless schmucky Janet's even dumber twin.

But she owed it to Reg Maundy to go along and support him. He was one of the few genuine showbiz leftovers she could call friend.

She'd have to go backstage: 'Reg! Daaarling, you were fabulous!' 'Marie! You were super!' 'Freddy! We must do lunch!'

Once upon a time she did kissie-kissies well. It was, after all, part of the price of the ticket to Showbiz Central. Stella knew when it was fitting to drop her drawers, bend over and think of England.

She arrived early for Rocky that night, figuring she'd get a few stiff Beefeaters into her in an uncrowded bar, then hide in a dark corner of the foyer. She thought, not for the first time, that she was in danger of turning into a clichéd paranoid spinster lady.

The bells rang. Stella shuddered, gulped and bolted into the darkening theatre. The stage looked suitably grotty and moody – all black and red and fog and shadows. High up in the flies were the large sets – a car chassis, a 1950s Coke machine, a Frankenstein Laboratory – which would, no doubt, fly in and out, up and down.

11

The lights dimmed. After 20 minutes or so, Reg came out like a perverted cool Joan Crawford and started howling 'Sweet Transvestite', looking 30 instead of the gorgeous 50 Stella knew him to be. *He's been working out*, Stella thought, *buffed, legs like a muscly chorus girl*. The crowd ate from his hand and even the determinedly morose Stella started humming along.

CREAK!

The fridge 25 feet above Reg detached from its moorings, plummeted down and landed smack on Reg with terrible authority. KEERACK! He'd been crushed by a Coke machine!

The band stopped playing. Brad and Magenta screamed. Janet vomited. Little Columbia fainted. A rivulet of blood that looked black in the stage lights glooped from under the Coke machine. Reg Maundy's black blood – who would have thought he had so much blood in him? – flowed over the side of the stage towards the audience.

'Ahhhh!' Screams and gurgles from the crowd set the cast off again. People started running for the door.

Rocky Horror, meet Marat/Sade. How d'ya do?

*

Within three minutes, the theatre was surrounded, cordoned off and locked up tight. Paramedics were overwhelmed with hysterical patrons. In remarkably short order, Specialists (Murder, Violent Crimes & Internal Probes) took charge and started taking statements. It was going to be some long long hours. Stella, who'd secreted a pint of Beefeater in her handbag, sat in a corner taking sips and waiting her turn. Of course she mourned poor Reg but he – and she – were troupers enough to know that while there are a million ignominious ways for an actor to die, no death could be more glorious than to cease upon the midnight, mid-song, in front of a full house.

*

Eventually, a tiny, sad Chinese murder investigator with a dark suit, dark eyes and shiny dark hair sat himself wearily next to Stella. He sized her up with a glance. Her hair long and thick, an almost unreal white, her face calm. Above average height. Quasi bohemian/faux-no-chic clothes. What his more worldly colleagues would call . . . curvy.

'Madam, I am Investigator Ng. I must apologise for the delay.'

Stella, in turn, took in Investigator Ng. Sallow face, eyes ringed with tired circles that looked almost like pain. He was so petite that, for a fleeting moment, Stella had the urge to put him in her handbag and let him sleep awhile.

He asked by rote, expecting the usual double negative: 'Did you notice anything out of the ordinary? Did you know the deceased?' His voice was soft, unaccented, cultured – the sort of man who spoke in full and grammatically precise sentences.

Stella thought back. Her mouth went dry – always her alert mind's signal to a dull body – wake up! think! you know this! *I know*, she thought. *I know.*

'Yes I did and yes I did,' said Stella. 'And perhaps I know who did it.'

She felt a flutter in her breast – a long-forgotten sensation. Excitement.

Investigator Ng, by contrast, felt almost nothing. In murder cases, someone who smells of gin and says 'I think I know who did it' is usually a time-squandering, attention-seeking, waste of air. Wearily, he lifted his eyes from his scribble pad to Stella's face.

Stella's own eyes were fixed on the foyer wall behind Ng's head, but her mind was roaming. The back alley leading to the stage door – when she was arriving early to Rocky and the bar for early drinks – Reg Maundy and his current boyfriend –

13

'I saw him arguing.'

Ng kept his stare fixed on her face as Stella slipped out of her trance. 'Arguing?'

'Yes, Investigator. With Tony. Tony Bunting. He's a bit of young rough trade. Reg adored him.'

'What was the problem?'

'I don't know.'

'Did Mr Bunting enter the theatre with Mr Maundy?'

'I don't know.'

Then suddenly she did know. 'Yes. Tony went in with Reg.'

'How do you know?'

'I don't *know*. It just seemed to me the fight was about to finish and they were about to make up.'

'How do you know?'

'I don't know that either. I . . .'

All at once her memory was like crystal, her senses sharp, chewing up clues. The smirk on Reg's face, victorious. Tony's slump, not so much sulky as eager. The position of their feet, pointing towards each other . . .

Stella felt alive, electric.

Ng sat back and watched her. He'd seen this – what? state of grace? – before. Ng's gift was logic but he wished he had more of this magic.

Finally Stella was ready. 'You see, Reg loved a bit of the rough. Sex-wise, I mean.'

Ng nodded, embarrassed.

'The rougher the better.'

Sage nod.

'Reg had been lapping up Tony's brutal butch bit for months. Reg was rich. Tony wasn't. Reg was Tony's meal ticket.'

Nod.

Stella took her time again, groping forward. 'The way

they ... looked. Reg was going to invite Tony in for a pre-show quickie. You know, make-up nookie.'

Nod.

'Reg loved messy all-over-the-floor-noisy-wham-bams, you know?'

Ng paled but smiled gamely.

'Reg snuck Tony in past the doorman. He's hiding some-where backstage, Investigator. Tough Tony Bunting is in Reg's dressing room.'

And he was, too.

Four minutes later, Stella, the small detective and a few uniforms found Tony Bunting in a cupboard underneath Reg's make-up table.

By chance, a freelance newspaper photographer sneaking round backstage happened to snap the million dollar shot: Stella looking on as the cops hauled terrified Tony out from the cupboard into the merciless world of a murder charge.

*

REG'S CRAZED GAY KILLER NABBED!

LADY SHOWBIZ DETECTIVE!

STELLA PENTANGELI, CRIMEBUSTER!

WHITE HAIR, STEEL FISTS!

*

It came out during the trial that Tough Tony and poor old Reg had fought about money but made up before the show. Then Tony got mad again and – never the sharpest knife in the drawer – climbed up into the wings and dropped the Coke machine on Reg. In panic, he hid in the cupboard, planning to

15

leave in the wee hours – and almost got away with murdering one of the stage's most beloved icons.

Alas, he had the bad luck to cross swords with Stella Pentangeli – newborn detective and scourge of showbiz evildoers everywhere.

*

SHOWBIZ! SHOWBIZ! SHOWBIZ! ONLINE!
THE PENTANGELI PAPERS *EXCLUSIVE*
REG MAUNDY MURDERED!
KILLER NABBED!
THE PENTANGELI PAPERS WERE THERE!
Reg Maundy, the brilliant highflying king of the musical theatre died tonight in a bizarre murder. His lover, Tony Bunting, is being questioned by police. I . . .

*

Angela Drumm, a singer/songwriter whom Stella adored above all seers and poets, once wrote:

> *How does it feel?*
> *How does it feel?*
> *This killer love?*
> *This killer love?*
>
> *How does it feel?*
> *How does it feel?*
> *Not too heavy?*
> *This killer love?*

The photo of Stella 'capturing' Tough Tony was perfect media fodder, and it flashed round the world. Stella realised that fate had handed her that fabled beast – a second chance. With

Reg's horrid onstage death, her ship had come in, piloted by Captain Luck and loaded to the gunwales with good fortune. If she played her cards right, Stella Pentangeli, struggling cyber-hack, could have a second famous career. If she made it this time, she vowed she'd use her second 15 minutes more wisely and well.

2.

nelson

Nelson J. Sharp was once one of the most gifted TV actors of his generation. He had forged himself in the white-hot bellows of ambition, devoting his young life to acting classes, elocution, dance, movement, gym. He spent many many nights in his room not – as his mother fondly hoped – engaged with pornography, but emoting crummy scripts from crummy soaps: *The Judases*, *Balls*, *Neighbourhood*, *Ocean Beach Fire Dept*. Didn't matter what the role was, Nelson did it, then did it again in the mirror. He'd play the insolent juvenile, the hard-as-nails sports coach, the village Romeo, the blind boy trapped in the mine, the worried mother, the doting grannie. 'Get it right, get it right, get it right!'

By the time Nelson turned 16, as luck would have it, he was gorgeous. He'd never been a victim of the adolescent hormones that poison the body and cook up zits, boils and blackheads, and his rise through the tele-ranks was swift. Nelson was, like King David of old, 'an lucky fellowe'.

If TV acting is appearing to be appealing while faking being real (and it is), Nelson had the world by the nuts. He found huge fame as Kyle the sensitive teen spunk motor mechanic in *The Young and the Naked*. For six years he basked in adoration.

Then the actor playing his wife was fired for wanting a pay rise. As soon as the wife left *TY&TN*, Nelson's character suddenly seemed . . . boring.

Partly because Nelson was taking mboké, the newest drug of choice, he was also looking . . . ugly.

Mboké was a severely enhanced version of artificial cocaine that got its nickname from 'more better cocaine'. The war inside Nelson's cells between the downers he used to kill the mboké and the mboké he used to kill the downers was starting to show. His finely chiselled face got a little puffy. His six-pack stomach got a little keggy. So, over poor Nelson's tears and protests and promises to go straight, *TY&TN* fired him.

'People will know I've been axed,' he moaned – and he was right. 'This will ruin my career!' he screamed – and he was right.

*

The only job Nelson could scavenge was as presenter on *Answer The Question!*, a quiz show. That lasted a month. They fired him because he looked . . .

evil.

He carried psychic baggage now. A neon question mark hung above his head. 'Why me, Lord, you bastard?' People looked into Nelson's face and saw not the handsome and talented star of yore but a bitter young creep.

Boring. Ugly. Evil. Bitter

How the mighty do fall.

What had happened to all that fame, all that glory? Was this it? Was he to be that most pathetic of creatures, the has-been, the ex-star, all the hyphenated half-shells he'd once scoffed at?

*

SHOWBIZ! SHOWBIZ! SHOWBIZ! ONLINE!
THE PENTANGELI PAPERS *EXCLUSIVE*
NELSON J. SHARP MUGGED IN ALLEGED
DRUG BUY!

Once he was an up and coming superstar but . . .

*

'What do we have here?' The voice was high and innocent like it belonged to a 13-year-old boy – which it did. The boy had two friends with him, aged maybe 15 and 19, but Nelson figured the high-voiced lad was the leader because he was the first to step forward and hit him. In the face. With a brick. The others followed suit.

Nelson went down and, as he went down, he knew he should never have come to this dangerous part of town at night. He had to, of course, since he needed the mboké before his body seized up.

'What do we have here?' The oldest boy echoed the youngest as he kicked Nelson's head.

Young hands reached into his pockets as he lay carefully still. They plucked out the drug money (400 dollars, borrowed) and were happy.

'Excellent!' said the first.

'Excellent!' said the second.

'Cool!' said the third.

Nelson guessed they would leave now, but the youngest one took another look at Nelson frozen with fear and shock on the ground. 'Shit! It's that smeg-head from *Answer The Question!*' Not too long ago, these thugs had been bright-eyed youngsters and lovers of TV. Now they had a chance to join in the wonderful world of showbiz by proxy – by beating the crap out of Nelson.

'Think you're better than . . .'

'I hate poofters who . . .'

'Think you're better than . . .'

'Answer *this* question, you . . .'

They stopped only when they heard the tired police siren heading their way – and with a final WHAP! THUD! SLAM! they rushed off with poor Nelson's blood on their boots and his money in their hands. Nelson knew he would never be this low again. 'Lord!' he screamed to the heavens, 'save me from myself and I will serve Thee! Helllpppp meeeee!!'

The ambos and the police rushed to him but Nelson hardly noticed. He was smiling. In that dark alley, on that night, on that piece of ground, Nelson J. Sharp, 23, had seen the face of YHWH. And God told Nelson he must save his soul. He must deliver His Word to showbiz. He must raise the holy, raze the evil and humble the proud.

'You will start My Work at The Fortnight,' YHWH rumbled.

'Yes Lord,' said Nelson the Prophet. 'I will go to The Fortnight.'

3.

the fortnight

Just days after she'd fingered Tough Tony for the *Rocky Horror Show* murder Stella found herself at The Fortnight.

The Fortnight had started in the 1970s as a small get-together of passionate theatre folk and quickly grew into a showbiz institution. Every year, in the autumnal glory of the first semester break at Bushy Creek University, in the woody university town of Bushy Creek in the high country, a couple of dozen actors, a dozen playwrights and half a dozen directors gathered to take over Faust Hall, a pseudo-Gothic residential college on the campus. They workshopped plays. Read, rewrote, staged and analysed plays.

During The Fortnight, lubricity oozed from the very walls and hung pungent in the air. Sleep was ever an optional extra. Once they had 700–800 guests. Nowadays, 100, tops. Loners, grannies, weirdos – all desperate to mingle with their showbiz betters.

Sex – bi, het, hom, omni. Liquor, speed, mboké, pills, ganja. Love, respect, hero-worship. Rampant egos, ideological fights and fisticuffs, feuds and grudges.

The Fortnight had it all. It was, in short, the perfect place for murder.

*

Ever since showbiz gave her the boot, Stella didn't do The Fortnight – ever – even though Artistic Director Jeddah Magnum sent her an invite every year. Stella's opinion was that theatre had become as relevant as bear baiting and cock fighting and the only theatre audiences left were thespic junkies who'd watch retards fuck mud as long as it was well reviewed and the tickets were expensive.

Naturally Stella kept these views to herself. She was the founder, editor and publisher of *The Pentangeli Papers*. How would people feel if she confessed that the most exciting thing she'd seen onstage in years was her friend Reg getting murdered?

But this year Stella was eager to ride the wave of publicity Reg's death had brought. And the staff of *The Pentangeli Papers* could manage without her. The entire staff was an insanely young gay volunteer called Terry Dear who could edit like an angel and, as important, knew his FTP (whatever that was) from his HTTP (whatever that was). All Stella knew was Terry waved something and, voila! there was *The Pentangeli Papers* on the net.

Stella thought about it. *A fortnight's holiday, free food, goss and – who knows? – maybe some sex. Please Lord.*

She packed a few books that she'd been meaning to devour: *The Gentford Handbook of Criminology*, *Introduction to Criminology*, *Criminal Profiling: An Introduction to Behavioural Evidence Analysis*, *Practical Homicide Investigation: Tactics, Procedures and Forensic Techniques*. Stella knew herself well enough to know she needed a passion or she'd wither and die. It looked like the private-eye gig was it.

*

Her battered yellow 80s V-dub clunked to a stop outside Faust Hall, which looked mysterious and solid in the morning light. Faust was a funny combo of an Oxfordesque three-storey dormitory and a 1970s offices/reception hall/bar. She had only two bags, one with enough clothing to scrape by for a fortnight and one with the books and three litre bottles of Beefeater gin carefully wrapped to prevent breakage and tell-tale tinkling.

'Ahhhh!' Jeddah Magnum swooped down on Stella from Faust Hall. Like many women in showbiz Promotion and Maintenance, Jeddah was fat. Not generously built or roomy or podgy. Fat. She had fat legs and arms and a big fat jolly belly. Her elbows were fat. She had many fat chins and a couple of them had chins. Only her delicate pink ears were not fat. Bright orange hair, a big lady's laugh and a big lady's talent for feuds. She never forgot a slight and always got her vengeance – a dish she liked cold.

Without people like her showbiz would have withered and died eons ago. There was surely a Jeddah Magnum in Athens at *Oedipus Rex*'s opening. A Jeddah helped Shakespeare make copies of *King Lear* and did the wind and storm noises. Jeddah, all 40 acres of her, was theatre's eternal handmaiden. She reached out two huge arms and suffocated Stella.

'You're looking *fabulous*!'

'You too, Jeddah! Thanks *so much* for the ticket!'

'Just give us plenty of bytes in that *wonderful* magazine of yours! Won't you?'

'Is a bear a Catholic? How's an entire issue of *The Pentangeli Papers* devoted to The Fortnight sound?'

'Like you're paying me back for a *bribe*!'

'You mean I'm *not*?!'

'Ha ha ha!'

'Ha ha ha!'

Ripping Stella's bags out of her hands Jeddah headed for the Oxford portion of Faust Hall. Stella followed, breathing a prayer that Jeddah would not drop her Beefeater bag.

*

It was a student crib all right. A tiny cubicle, half-concrete, half-chipboard, on the second story of the residential block. A desk. Cheap. A chair. Cheap. A washbasin. A single bed. The student tenant had wisely taken everything personal out except for a poster, blue-tacked on the wall, of suicidal-looking rock star Kurt Cobain – gorgeous, grubby, mother-starved.

'Darling, you *do* know you're on at six?'

Stella stared at Jeddah vacantly trying to get a fix on what she was saying.

'On what?'

'You're giving a seminar tomorrow night. At six.'

Stella went green. 'You mean – *speak?*'

'It was in the invitation I sent you,' Jeddah said firmly. 'The topic is "Fame! Stardust or Bullshit?".'

Stella would have preferred to suffer poor Reg Maundy's fate than to speak in public. The very thought of it sent her scurrying to the washbasin to throw up while Jeddah clucked and oo-ed behind her.

'Stells?'

'(vomit)'

'Relax. It'll only be the two of you.'

'Who?'

'You and Lou.'

Lou? She turned greenly towards Jeddah. 'Lou *Google?*'

'It was in the invitation I sent you. He's the other special guest.'

A seminar? In the same room as Lou? Every so often she still cursed the Fates that she and Lou Google were on the same *planet*.

'I can't do it, Jeddah. I won't. Especially not with Lou fucking Google.'

Jeddah unzipped Stella's bag, went unerringly to the stash, took out a bottle of Beefeater, filled two shot glasses, handed one to Stella and they both skolled – each thirsty in her own way. Stella sat on the bed, Jeddah on a cheap chair, her buttocks cascading down either side.

'It's not on until tomorrow, darling. Don't be such a drama queen.'

'Great! That gives me another' – she glanced at her watch – 'twenty-eight hours to sweat.'

'But Stells, you've been on TV and everything.'

'TV's not public speaking. It's diarrhoeic masturbation.'

'And so is *this* darling. It's only an hour or two. Lou's a pussycat these days. You're a big girl now – and speaking in public's like speaking in private only more crowded.'

Jeddah would never have stayed a handmaiden had she undue sympathy for the weaknesses of others. Notice of the seminar with Stella Pentangeli and Lou Google was *printed* in the brochures. The seminar was *advertised* on the Faust Hall noticeboard. She, Jeddah Magnum, had *said* there was to be a seminar with Stella Pentangeli and Lou Google and as God was her witness, there *would* be a seminar with Stella Pentangeli and Lou Google. On 'Fame! Stardust or Bullshit?', a debate on the value of the star system in modern showbiz.

Thus each played the part nature had assigned them. Stella allowed herself to be cajoled and flattered and Jeddah the Handmaiden, as ever, got her own way by talking, talking, talking.

'Okay, okay,' Stella said. 'I'll do it and if Lou gives me a hard time I'll hack off his balls.'

Jeddah smiled, atta-girl-ed, laughed at Stella's *bon mot*, poured anothery, then moved onto other things. Gossip.

'Poor Reg. Still, he went out in style, didn't he?' said Jeddah.

'He would have wanted it that way.'

'Yes.'

'Yes.'

'Why do old queens take up with rough trade and then whinge when the rough trade beats them up?'

'And leaves them flat. In Reg's case, literally.'

They laughed immoderately as Beefeater flooded their blood. Sorrow has its place but so does mirth. Jeddah stood. 'Must dash, darling. People to bleat and greet.'

'I might have a little nap.'

'I'll make sure you're woken in plenty of time for the Grand Reading.'

Stella lay back on the bed and . . .

Crash!

*

The sexiest black actor in recent history was Emu Gentle. When *The Pentangeli Papers* devoted an issue to him, the hits and subs soared. He was too good to be real. The Gent was funny, savvy and gorgeous: shiny midnight skin, tall, lithe, muscly, perfect-toothed. He was 23, could sing like an angel, played guitar like a rock star. Women threw themselves at his feet and groped higher. Men loved his self-deprecating humour and the joy he took in what he'd accomplished. The Gent had first appeared as a teenage tracker in *Alligator Man* – a surprise worldwide hit – and stole every scene he was in. He was offered Hollywood roles and took a few at many millions of dollars per. *Mad Max 5*, *Moulin Rouge Encore Une Fois*, *Othello* et al. Then he pocketed the money and came home.

'I'm rich enough,' he said. 'I did the movie star bit. Now it's time to help my brothers and sisters.' Was it any wonder he went through the hearts of females like grease through geese – that he could have had any of them with a wave of his pink-palmed and kingly hand?

27

*

Stella woke with a start. Huh? She was in a crowded, smoky bar. She was sexy. Voluptuous. Winnable. Emu Gentle was in skin jeans and a white silk shirt that hugged his black chest. He came over to her and they kissed. In front of the crowd he lifted her on to the bar, hands working her buttons, and . . .

Crash!

*

Stella woke with another start. They were in her apartment and she and The Gent were naked and unashamed. His skin shone, hers glowed, and their bodies joined and parted, joined and parted. He was hard and she was wet, and now he moaned her name – 'Stelllllaaaa!' She bit her tongue to stop screaming as she started to orgasm and . . .

Crash!

*

Stella woke up and looked around. She was in her cubicle. The door opened and in front of her stood Emu Gentle, his dark silky body clad only in a white towel. But she was sick of dreams. 'Piss off!'

'Pardon me,' said The Gent, 'I thought this was my room.'

'Yeah, yeah. If you're real, why don't you drop the towel, bring that shlong over here and fuck me stupid?'

Long surprised silence. Then Stella watched as Emu fled, making sure – gent that he was – her door was locked properly this time.

Hours later, she realised that when she told Emu Gentle to fuck her stupid, that bit wasn't a dream. It was real life.

Oy.

4.

blackout.
sound of gunshot

Tradition dictated that, before the Welcome Dinner in the Grand Dining Hall, the actors, directors, playwrights, guests and observers should gather in the University of Bushy Creek's Majestic Theatre for the Grand Reading. Even though The Fortnight adhered strictly to the notion that all plays are created equal, some plays were more equal. The Grand Reading play was odds-on favourite to be snapped up a by major theatre company.

In the setting sun the campus was chilly and fantastically beautiful. The whole pack of Fortnighters wandered through the failing light towards the Majestic Theatre. Jeddah had her acolytes, Emu his groupies. Even Stella had a few fans — those perspicacious enough to sense Stella's star of fame was on the rise again. Loners and couples made up the rest of the throng.

Stella was hungover and haggard. She spotted Emu, scurried over to him and — to the groupies' chagrin — hustled him away from the mob. 'Mr Gentle, I'm so sorry . . . about this afternoon.'

'No problems, Miss Pentangeli. Really.'

'It's just that when I told you to go away I thought you were a ghost.'

He grinned wickedly. 'And what about the bit where I was supposed to drop my towel, bring my shlong over and fuck you stupid?'

Stella grinned queasily. 'I thought I was dreaming.'

'I wish *I* had dreams like that.'

'I . . .'

'Listen, Miss Pentangeli, I've always liked and admired your work. Truly, really, it's forgotten. There's just one problem.'

'What?'

He took her hand and kissed it. 'The problem is my friends call me Emu. So start being my friend.'

Oh God, why weren't there a million men like Emu?

*

Cordelia Heath was known as a fine actor, the tragic saviour of Robbie George, a striking, stunning piece of old New Left fire and beauty – and now she had added playwrighting to her list of accomplishments. When it was announced that Cordelia Heath's first play had been chosen for the Grand Reading, jealousy vied with awe.

'A Grand Reading Play? Cordelia Heath?'

'She's so beautiful. She's so clever. Cordelia can do *anything*.'

'I bet the play's a turkey.'

'I bet it's *brilliant*!'

The stage had always been Cordelia's true love. It was there she'd always been on fire. The trouble was she was almost never on the stage since she was as purist about popular theatre as she was about everything else. She had so routinely and vociferously knocked back stage offers from the majors that she was seldom asked these days, and were she to be asked she'd likely tell them to shove it or, worse, spend a week insulting the director for being racist, ageist, sexist, anti-gay – and get fired.

In theory, then, everyone was rooting for Cordelia's play. In practice, there were only a few who didn't carry some degree of hope that the play would be a stinkeroonie. As Gore Vidal once almost said: a man needs not only to win, he also needs his friends to fail.

*

The Majestic Theatre seated 499 and was perfect for the Grand Reading. It had class. It had been the original Bushy Creek Majestic Cinema in the 1940s. When the town had been subsumed by the nascent university, it had been restored as the uni playhouse.

At 5.10 exactly, Jeddah shut and locked the doors. She insisted upon punctuality in all matters Fortnight. She introduced the pale but composed author.

'You all know Cordelia Heath.' Polite applause. 'This is her first play. It's titled "Midwinter dreams of a dead black man". Please remember this is a first reading only and is still to be workshopped.' She motioned offstage and the actors, led by Emu Gentle, came onstage, sat down on a row of chairs and began.

*

pg 1. Scene One.
The riverside.
Benjamin Franco, a Black Man, enters, talking to himself.
Ben: She talking to me. Angel. You're like what they call a comet.
You're a messenger and I'm a-lookin' at ya in the lazy clouds.

pg 15.
Ben: (sings)
I know who I am
I know what I is
I'm black and I'm proud

Mind your own biz (ness)
I'm a B.L.A.C.K. man.
Yeah.

My mother was black
My daddy was white
He taught me to fear
She taught me to fight.
I'm a B.L.A.C.K. man.
Yeah.

pg 16. Scene Nine.
The rich man's kitchen. Mary and Ben enter, in love.
Mary: Alas my love you'd do me wrong if you throw me away.
Ben: Yeah dat'd be rude.
Mary: I've been in love with you so very very long.
Ben: Me too. I loves your company.
They kiss.

pg 57. Scene Twenty.
Ben takes a gun from the desk drawer, puts it to his head.
Ben: I can't live this way no more. Mary, I'm coming home.
As he is about to blow his brains out . . .
Blackout. Sound of gunshot.
The End.

*

There wasn't a dry eye in the house. Cordelia's unexpectedly brilliant first play was an unmitigated triumph. It told, in 90 minutes — 20 short scenes, a dozen songs — the story of a love affair between Benjamin Franco, a black man, and Mary St Mary, a white woman, during the late 19th century. At the very start of the play, Mary is killed by the racist town mob. Ben then falls into a series of dreams which depict various scenes from his life and strange post-modern flashes of what appear to be non-sensical snatches of talk and song and action. Ben awakens from the dream and, unable to stand life without Mary, kills himself.

Jeddah asked for comments. Cordelia sat humble yet triumphant.

Opined one regular Fortnighter who was, admittedly, nuts: 'It's one of those works of art that manages to contain the world within a sentence and the entire universe within each page and so we, the fourth wall of the stage, are the lucky, the privileged few able to help contain the miracle.' The rest were more succinct, forgetting their earlier unworthy prognostications of failure.

'A masterpiece.'

'Awesome.'

'A new form, for Chrissakes! Pre-post-post-modern perfection.'

Emu Gentle waited for someone – anyone – to point out that the play was *awful*! Not only was there no structure, the dialogue was laughable and the only 'theme' seemed to be that it's best if blacks die to expunge the sins of the white man. This fatuous and foolish Uncle Tom/Christ stereotype had run ad nauseam through Western culture for 200 years. When in doubt, kill off the coloured folk in the last act. Hell, Emu had thought the play was a comedy when he'd first read it. During the reading he'd kept waiting for the laughs to start, but this crew not only took it seriously, they thought it was brilliant!

Oy.

*

Jeddah cut short the hallelujahs and escorted Cordelia – surrounded by a throng of instant groupies – back along the dark path to Faust Hall and the Opening Night Dinner.

33

*

The vast dining hall held 13, 14 tables, each of which could hold 8 people. This meant the guests could arrange themselves like island nation states around the room and be guaranteed a measure of independence and sovereignty.

Setting up state next to the Gent was a 17-year-old redhead who had made sure never to stray far from his side as they walked to the hall under chilly stars.

'Hi. My name's Lucy. Lucy Sky. I'm a drama student. And I write songs and sing. Mainly blues and gospel and stuff. This is going to be such *fun*.'

Even at her tender age, Lucy Sky regarded showbiz as a blood sport. Her studies in Biology had taught her that sweet little chirping birdies are actually hunting for bugs or attacking other birds and shitting everywhere. Darwin called nature 'red in tooth and claw' and Lucy applied that same definition to her ambition. Birds killing and being killed. Baby birds still inside their shells being chewed up by snakes. Lucy found all this thrilling and comforting.

She watched as Emu turned to her and tried to smile. His mind was plainly elsewhere. Gee, the redhead thought, he seems angry.

*

Emu Gentle was too sophisticated, too *gentlemanly*, to take Lucy's flirtations seriously. The Gent understood the seductive power of fame and to abuse that power for sexual conquest would be, to his mind, a form of rape. Lucy was loamy, concupiscent, ripe and ready, but Oh Lordie! was she young and dumb.

Emu owed it to his honour to think of his wife and children and not of his sexual gratification. Instead, having made sure that Cordelia Heath was on the other side of the room, he ventured a few reasoned words about the manifest failures of 'Midwinter dreams of a dead black man'.

'It's like they found the most doctrinaire dodo, the Mayor of Clichéville, and got him to write a hunk of junk. All blacks good, all whites bad.'

All the while Lucy was pretending to listen, she was thinking how to pork him.

*

Jeddah Magnum — at the table behind Emy and Lucy — listened and grew more incensed at every word. 'Midwinter dreams of a dead black man' was *not* a joke, *not* a liberal wank, *not* a play that should be buried at sea. She had chosen this play! Jeddah's shaky finances — her very reputation — depended on this seminal new work. *Plus*: what if someone heard Emu babbling and it got into the media? She might as well haul her massive frame onto a highway during a dense fog and pray for traffic. No, no, no. Emu Gentle was doing what *men* had done all through history — scorning women artists, putting them in their place. *Typical!*

The young slut waved her tits and teeth around. *Typical!*

As Jeddah fumed behind his back, Emu kept talking. Had his tongue been a machine pistol and his words bullets, he could not have done a better job of shooting himself between the eyes.

5.

eros #1

Lucy slept the sleep of the superior. She'd known from the time she could regard herself in any convenient shiny surface that she was special.

She had taken up piano and guitar and song writing early. Mummy and Daddy paid. She would sing her songs to anyone who'd listen. She learnt to summon magic from the piano and the acoustic guitar. Her voice had grown full, mature, ready. She knew she wasn't much of a lyricist but she could write tunes that broke your heart or got your feet twitching.

She was young, beautiful, sexy, talented and full of confidence. What else did anyone need to get to the top? Then fate had shown her an article in the paper about The Fortnight and she knew instantly that this could be a back door to the hotel that housed the stairway to the stars.

*

One of the benefits of running The Fortnight was the free food and Jeddah always got hungriest at night.

She picked up the knife. It was large and gleaming with a dark polished wooden handle – the sort of slicer-dicer popular in teenage horror flicks. She had brought it from her caravan park home just outside Bushy Creek and was busy with a leg of ham and a pound of French brie taken from the giant Faust Hall pantry. She severed generous portions of meat and cheese. Yummy.

Jeddah wolfed down the food, then looked at the dildo half-nestling under her pillow. She moved to the bed, picked it up, then caressed her pale pink flesh.

Eros would be on the prowl tonight. Faust Hall was starting to Fortnight.

Eros, my arse.

She threw the dildo away. It hit the door with a thump and bounced to the floor where it belonged. She was the Nurse in a Shakespeare sex comedy, except she was fatter and uglier. While Romeo and Juliet were making love, Nurse Jeddah would be in her concrete bunker with her fucking dildo. The enchanted isle of Eros, Faust Hall, with its scores of French farce doors, was a barren desert to her.

Tears welled. Wearily she moved to the door, bent and picked up her one companion – a pink and obscene piece of grooved rubber. At least she'd sleep. But first, some more ham and a nice slice of brie.

6.

fame! stardust or bullshit?

There's a joke about an old guy in a circus who's demoted to a new job—walking behind the elephant with a spade and a bucket and shovelling the shit into the bucket. All day, every day. Stinking filthy steaming elephant poo. And every day as he shovels, he whinges and bitches and gnashes his teeth. One day a young man comes up to him and says: 'If you hate it so much, why don't you just leave?' And the old guy looks at the kid shocked and mortified and says: 'And quit *showbizness*?' For most people that's the whole truth of the biz. The shit piles up and it never stops but we keep shovelling until we die.

Lou Google was never one to shovel shit. Lou Google was one of the very few people in history who could claim to have wrestled showbiz to the ground, kicked her in the teeth, made her squeal for mercy, then stolen her purse. Lou Google had Made It Big. From the very start Lou had been determined to Make It Big in something.

His parents divorced when he was an infant, and his beautiful mother never showed a desire to work again or marry rich again. Consequently Lou suffered from growing up in a world where everyone who mattered was better off than him. He went to the Right Schools and moved in the Right Circles but the lack of that crucial extra income from his father – now on his second wife, now his third, now a 19-year-old mistress – meant that Lou was patronised by his well-off classmates and the rich and leggy daughters of the upper middle classes. In the merciless hierarchy of childhood, Lou was, if not a bottom feeder, then a subtle reminder of which direction the bottom was and how much nicer it was up top.

Outside he smiled. Inside he raged. Mankind is replete with childhoods like Lou's. Some kids go under, most shrug it off, a few become serial killers or politicians. Lou went into showbiz. His keenly honed instinct for self-preservation picked up the notion very early that fame was as good as money until money came along. TV was where both fame and money were quickly to hand.

In anyone who wasn't as irrevocably ignoble as Lou Google, there would have been something magnificent in the boy's fierce dedication to learning his craft. But his was less the muscular quest of a driven artist than it was the panic of a drowning boy groping for a lifesaver. He taught himself the basics of writing, directing and all the minor corners of TV. He swept studio floors, made coffee for the suits, kept keeping on.

By the time he was 23 he was a suit at Channel 4, where he learnt how to cut throats, protect his butt, cover his tracks. He proved himself adept at picking local shows that might last longer than the time it took bored watchers to hit the remote button. His power and influence grew and by 32 he found himself in a large corner office able to hire and fire. They rabbits, he fox. 'Oh Lord! Power at last! Let the rage out of the cage!' The suckers on the lower rungs saw nothing but Lou's arse.

Rage. It's perhaps the main attribute needed in a TV executive.

*

Day Two of The Fortnight, Lou sat with a carefully bruised book on Stanislavsky at a picnic table in the Faust Hall gardens – his brown hair shaggy and shiny and freshly cut, his face tanned just so, his gym-toned body not so much buffed, as polished. He knew he looked good. He had no fear of public speaking. Quite the contrary, he had offered – he always offered – to do a seminar for free at The Fortnight and Jeddah, as always, eagerly took him up on it.

Lou got his presence and status advertised early and loud. Which was good. Lou was astute enough to realise that, however powerful he was in his world, at The Fortnight he was just an expensively dressed coiffed and manicured TV suit, to be scorned by the hothouse young. And the hothouse young were the reason Lou was here. Specifically the hothouse young women.

'Fame! Stardust or Bullshit?', 'Theatre, Television and Art', 'Come Clean! Soaps Suck!', 'Kids' Drama – Suffer The Little Children', whatever, didn't matter, make it up. Each year these dumb seminars guaranteed that the young women Lou was interested in would get him on their radar. Lou's tastes were specific and not very original. He liked them young, ripe and pretty with an edge of the neurotic. He wanted, in short, the girls who'd knocked him back in his moneyless youth and The Fortnight once served them up by the truckload.

As Lou had said seductively to more than one pretty young thing: 'The future can be a thankless place with nothing but old faded dreams and no money in the bank.' In Lou's eyes, these hothouse Fortnighters were the younger sisters of the painted and eager chickie-babes who inhabited TV – the soap stars and wannabes, the current affairs cuties, the PAs, the AMWs (actress/model/whatevers). They fell into bed in his cubicle every year like clockwork.

40

*

A very pretty redheaded Fortnight girl, perhaps 16 or 17, dressed in baggy jeans and a NY Yankees jumper, looked at him and clocked that he was 35, 40. He was good looking in an Al Pacino way but too old.

Lou could see her at the edge of his eye and knew what she was thinking. He smiled to himself. She'll come round. I'll fuck her stupid.

The young redhead – hidden behind the Faust Hall windows – reappraised Lou. When he smiled to himself like that, he was handsome.

*

Seminar time. In the Main Hall, Lucy Sky was smugly patting herself on the back for her foresight in saving her pennies to come to The Fortnight. It was just about already worth it – for barely a metre away from her chair sat Emu Gentle, her personal hero as an actor, a fighter for his people, and a pin-up stud muffin. Behind her, near the door was Nelson J. Sharp, the dork who used to be on *Answer The Question!* a year or two ago and who got found in some alley all beaten up. The hungover looking woman who'd just entered was Stella Pentangeli, the quote unquote lady showbiz detective who'd solved some murder of some old actor doing *Rocky*. Lucy would have been surprised (or indifferent) to learn Stella had been a player way before she had been born. That was then. This is now.

Lucy caught a few old dudes and some hotties checking her out and smiled to herself. She changed seats and sat next to Emu.

'Hi.'

'Hey.'

Oh yeah! thought Lucy.

*

When Lou was 22 and Stella was at the height of her power, she'd seen a new soap called *The Homicide Boys* which, she noted, the wunderkind Louis Google had written. She'd praised it in her weekly column and, such was her juice, given Lou's career a boost just at the right time.

Lou had made it his business to bump into Stella at her journo bar hangout. He thanked her, bought her a drink and asked if he could see her home.

'You? Me? You're a TV hack!'

'Ha ha ha' went her florid journo friends. In the complicated equation that is youth and ego and the needy greed of the half-loved, Lou had been hit in several places. Stella had foolishly pulled down his pants in front of the whole class to show them how tiny his dick was.

Silly Stella.

Lou's ears turned red and he headed for the door. As the baboon laughter followed him into the night, Stella sensed through the gin that she'd made herself an enemy. Truth be told, if she hadn't been drinking with her buddies when Lou approached her, she would have been tempted to take him home. She was feeling the first early stirrings of mortality. A hard-bodied boy like Louis Google might be just what she'd needed on this warm drunken night.

*

Lou scowled as Stella made her anxious way to the front of the 100-strong throng and took her edgy seat next to a beaming Jeddah.

'Fame! Stardust or Bullshit?'

Lou had led off, but his timing was awry. This was because, in spite of his best efforts, Stella never left the periphery of his vision. He was surprised at how angry at her he still was, even after all these years. And he was angry with himself for being angry. Surely a Stella Pentangeli was beneath him now?

Stella, in turn was real real angry with him. She was astute enough not to blame one event or person for the outrageous fortunes of her life but, as near as dammit, Lou Google held a portion of that blame in his perfectly manicured hands.

For debating purposes, Lou took the position that there was no art without commerce, so stars were good because they drew an audience to 'the product'.

On any other day with any other speaker, Stella would have agreed wholeheartedly but, because it was shitface Google, she argued that the star system was inimical to art, had ruined Hollywood and turned TV into an intellectual kindergarten.

Lou begged to differ. Blah blah blah.

They went at it hammer and tongs and the usual handful of observers who could be relied upon to wait bovine-like for a chance to say their bit couldn't get a word in. Not during, nor after.

The seminar solved nothing, resolved nothing, meant nothing — but it made for good theatre.

*

Lucy was surprised, then amused, then bored. She didn't want to hear old people talk. She wanted to be one of the stars these people were talking about.

*

Nelson agreed with Stella. Of course stars were an Evil Thing. Look what fame and stardom and showbiz had done to him.

'Chastise and rebuke. Humble the proud. Slay the mighty.' YHWH whispered this and more in his ear.

43

*

Emu Gentle dropped into a mild trance deeply sorry he'd agreed to come to this Fortnight wank.

*

Cordelia Heath – tall, Amazonian, Goddessy and now star of The Fortnight – entered ostentatiously late. Natch.

*

After 90 minutes, Jeddah wound it up.

*

The tiny Faust Hall Bar was full of Fortnighters. Those in the know were surprised indeed to see Lou Google, TV supremo scum, and Stella Pentangeli, has-been critic and half-arsed private eye, huddled in a corner table, looking for all the world like they were enjoying each other's company. He talking, she laughing delighted.

Lucy was a tad miffed. Earlier, after she found out who Lou was, she had come onto him. Pretending ignorance, exuding innocence, she had started chatting excitedly. 'Hi. My name's Lucy. Lucy Sky. I'm a drama student. And I write songs and sing. Mainly blues and gospel and stuff. This is going to be such *fun*.'

And there he was after the old boring chick.

She looked around for Emu but he'd split. Shit.

*

Forty minutes later. Stella and Lou lip-locked outside her room. Whoosh. Inside. They shred their clothes, fall on the bed.

'Oh my God!'

'Yes!'

'*Why* did we wait so long?'

'Baby!'

'Yes!'

There is a thin line between love and hate, between lust and loathing and Lou and Stella have crossed it very noisily indeed.

'Oh my God!'

'Yes!'

'Why did we wait so long?'

'Baby! Baby! Baby!'

'Yes! Yes! Yes!'

'Baby! Baby! Baby!'

'Yes! Yes! Yes!'

'Oh my God!'

7.

body

It sounded like the end of the world but it was just some birds fighting and cacking in the trees outside – not so much greeting the day as scaring the shit out of it. Through the double glaze pane above her bed, Stella saw it was a cold sunny morning and nature was all over the place.

'Ahhh!' she gasped. Someone was hidden way under the covers next to her. *Oh yeah. Lou Google. Now how the hell did that happen?*

'Lou?' No response. He was stiff and cold. Typical.

'Lou?'

Dead to the world. Men. She got up, shy, climbed quickly into her towel robe and put on the kettle. She figured that since the shower cubicles were just down the hall, once she woke Lou up they could maybe have a shower together. Maybe even . . .

. . . do it again.

From the woofy whiff she'd picked up when she got out of bed, he sure could use a shower. The kettle boiled.

'Lou? Coffee?' She shook him gently but it was like he'd deliberately steeled himself against her touch. *Fuck this.* She tossed the blanket aside and . . .

'Ahhh!'

Stella found herself looking into a blue-black face with a thick black tongue protruding from white lips. Yellowed eyes stared blankly back at her. Lou's right arm lay naturally at his side, but his left arm was crooked in a stiff semi-Nazi salute, the hand clenched into a claw. One finger was pointing at a wicked kitchen knife stuck in his chest just right of his left nipple. The knife was *large* with a dark polished wooden handle. Stella grabbed it, thinking she'd pull it out, then realised what she was touching and recoiled from the bed. She couldn't help but think this was a joke – a parody of the horse head scene in *The Godfather* – but knew it wasn't.

*

The Bushy Creek uniforms were clearly out of their depth. Bushy Creek was a small town and the local area commander couldn't remember the last non-natural death that wasn't a road trauma or a domestic. He moved everybody into the Dining Hall and went straight to the Prime Witness.

'Miss Pentagon,' the commander began.

'Pentangeli.'

'Miss Pentangeli, an investigator is on the way down from the city. You're to stay dressed in that robe.'

'Why?'

'Standard procedure.'

'Bullshit. I'm not hanging round half-naked.'

With that – not thinking clearly – Stella took off the robe and climbed into panties, slacks and a sloppy joe she'd brought down from her bedroom. Only the area commander looked away shyly. The Fortnighters and the uniforms caught an eyeful and that was fine with them. The commander turned to Jeddah.

'I need to borrow a small room, Miss Magnum.'

'Certainly, Commander,' said Jeddah.

47

The miffed-at-being-disobeyed commander put shameless Stella into 'sequestration' in the music room as punishment and tried to figure out what to do until the big city investigators arrived.

*

The state's murder unit is on the eleventh floor of One Police Towers. Its full title is Specialists MVC&IP (Murder, Violent Crimes and Internal Probes) and, whatever you called it, Investigator Ng was the king of it. The best.

MVC&IP sent Investigator Ng in spite of his objections. He wanted nothing to do with the Pentangeli woman. In his modest way, Ng resented the amount of attention she'd received over the '*Rocky Horror Show* Murder'. She'd been a useful witness who'd helped with enquiries, but that was all.

'Ng, you're going. A murder at The Fortnight, with all them famous names is automatically an SOD, you know that,' said Hawkeye – Unit Commander and Ng's immediate superior. SOD was unit slang for a Solve Or Die, which meant the heavy hitters in police and politics needed a quick result.

Ng looked at Hawkeye and marvelled. If society had created so many miracles over the centuries, why couldn't it get glass eyes quite right? The boss's gelatinous one was bloodshot blue, and never stopped darting irritably around. The glass one was pristine blue, always faced rigidly front.

'Take any Specialists you want, take a lab team. Just get a result,' said Hawkeye. 'And cheer up. You might get lucky. Maybe that Pentangeli broad did it.'

*

Stella was tinkling away at 'Chopsticks' on a fine old Steinway when an ancient doctor knocked and entered with the commander.

The doctor prescribed Stella some valium immediately. He knew women. He knew their frailty and he was one of the old school who believed in pills the way his forebears believed in leeches and bloodletting.

'I'll have to take some blood, I'm afraid.'

'Okay.'

He took the blood.

'And some fingernail scrapings,' the commander added.

'Why?'

'Standard procedure.'

The doctor took some scrapings.

'Oh, and you're not to take a shower,' the commander said.

'Why not?'

'Well, we'll be needing semen and pubic hair samples.'

'I haven't been raped, you moron. Lou's semen's in a used condom back in my room.'

The mortified commander struggled to speak. 'Now see here . . .'

But the doctor stopped him. He understood. She was frail. He led the commander away. Stella heard the door lock behind them.

For the next several hours, only Jeddah was allowed to enter with cups of very hot very sweet tea and scones with jam. She was accompanied by a uniform and was under strict instructions not to speak to the 'sequestree'.

By her third visit Jeddah had decided to ignore the instructions. She comforted Stella, who seemed to be in shock or denial. Jeddah had the impression that Stella hadn't grasped the notion that she might well have been killed too.

Unless, of course, *Stella* did it.

*

When Investigator Ng walked into the music room, Stella started up right away. 'I want a shower! Goddamnit!'

Ng waved a benign hand. 'Of course. Why haven't you had one?'

'The local head cretin wouldn't let me.'

'But that is silly. This is not a rape,' said clever Ng, thus signalling to Stella that they were old pals, war buddies. She shouldn't listen to these hicks. Just to him. Her friend, Mr Ng.

Ten minutes later, a freshly scrubbed Stella returned.

'Good to see you, Ms Pentangeli,' said Ng, doing his best to mean it.

'And you, Investigator,' said Stella.

Ng was not a great one for modern technology. He would not use a mobile phone, for instance, convinced that they would cause brain cancer, and was astounded at the numbers of people who used them with such insouciance. But he loved his tiny digicam and delighted in scoping every crime scene with it.

'Present in the room are Investigator Ng N.G. and Miss Stella Pentangeli P.E.N.T.A.G.E.L.I. I am recording this on a MiniCam 3000 with time and date clearly stamped. Copies of this videotape will be supplied on valid request. Now, Miss Pentangeli, how long have you known the client?'

'Client?'

'Mr [checks notebook] Google.'

'About fifteen years.'

'That's how long you knew Reg Maundy, if memory serves.'

All her life, Stella had felt intimidated by authority. When she was driving a car, the sight of a cop in her rear vision would send her heart pittering. No longer. 'Investigator, I'm not a psycho who bumps off friends when I get bored with them.'

'Pity. It'd make this job so much easier.'

Stella looked at him. He'd made a joke, she thought, but she wasn't sure. His face was unreadable. Last time they'd met, Ng had looked exhausted. Stella had put it down to the weariness of the hour and the number of people to be questioned. This time he just looked sad.

'But Mr Google *wasn't* a friend, was he?' Ng went on. 'A little bird whispered in my ear that you and the client had been enemies for years.'

Stella looked at him. *How the hell does he know? He just got here.*

'Was this "little bird" four hundred pounds with orange hair?'

'You were . . . with the client last night, I gather?'

The Investigator's voice was smooth. Stella knew what he was doing. If you're a cop you never answer questions, you ask them. Make the bad guys feed you.

'I was horny I guess.'

Jesus, he's blushing!

Ng face was impassive but Stella was right. He was red to the roots of his hair.

'Look, Investigator Ng, I don't know why Lou and I ended up in bed. He was a pig. But from what I can remember about last night, I enjoyed it.'

'You were drunk?'

'I must have been. Drunker than I thought, anyway. I was horn – I was open to persuasion.'

Ng knew many of the weird contortions of the human heart but it surprised him that Stella and the client corpse had gone from life-long enmity to sex. But, given all the liquor they had found in Stella's room, it was understandable. Indeed, she could have made love, woken up, seen the client, forgot she liked him, killed him, gone back to sleep and forgotten all about it.

Ng's forensics team was already at work in the Faust Hall sick bay field-testing the knife, probing the residue from under Stella's fingernails, sniffing the clues.

He started easy. 'Why were your fingerprints on the knife?'

'I tried to pull it out of Lou's chest.'

'Oh, of course.' From his tone, he might as well have said, 'Were you a born liar or did you study for a deception diploma?' He went on. 'People might well think you murdered the client, Miss Pentangeli.'

'Me?'

'Otherwise it makes no sense. How did the murderer get in? How did he kill the client without waking you?' He smiled at her with all the considerable melancholy he could muster, as if begging her to help him out here, to show him the folly of his thinking, to clear her good name. Or better yet – to confess.

Ng continued sadly. 'Then, of course, there is the dirt.'

'Dirt?'

'It came from the forest. Our specialists found it. Specks were embedded in your carpet.'

The Bushy Creek Forest National Park was 200 metres from Faust Hall and formed a natural boundary fence for the university. At first glance, it appeared to be a luxuriant little nook but, in fact, Bushy Creek Forest National Park stretched for scores of kilometres left, right and back.

'Dirt.' said Stella coolly. 'So?'

'So we checked, Miss Pentangeli. Since you arrived, you haven't been to the forest.'

'I hate the outdoors. I'm at two with nature.'

'You could have sneaked out to the forest while the client slept.'

'Why would I sneak out to the forest, Investigator?' Stella was getting pissed off.

'To fetch the knife.'

Stella's mouth went dry. Her subconscious was kicking her arse. 'Did you find any dirt on my shoes?'

Stella caught the flicker in Ng's eye. 'Er, no. Just in the carpet.'

It was worth a try, Ng thought resignedly. She was right, of course. The traces of dirt in the carpet actually *helped* her argument that there was a third person in the murder room.

Ng looks so pathetic, thought Stella. But another voice warned: Don't misjudge him. He's sharp. He's dangerous. He plays dirty.

'Do you take drugs? Sleeping pills? Tranquillisers?'

'Who doesn't?'

'Do you take TranQuax?'

'No.'

'Are you sure?'

'Of course I'm sure!'

TranQuax – tranks, pants-down pills, date-rape specials – were a barbiturate very popular in showbiz circles. The girls and boys took it for the pleasures of nodding off into soup and bouncing off walls while giggling. The older boys and girls used it for oblivion, or to lower the often commendable reluctance of a potential sex partner.

Ng consulted a piece of paper. 'Your blood test this morning showed high to very high levels of TranQuax. Three standard doses.'

The thought hit Stella and lit up her eyes. 'Of course! That's why I was so horny. Lou slipped tranks into my drink. I would have rooted a horse!'

Ng blushed. Some MVC&IP female police talked dirty too, but he could never get used to it.

Stella had another thought. 'And *that's* why I could sleep through the murder! I was off my face.'

Ng reached into his pocket, took out a small plastic baggie containing perhaps 50 white pills and showed them to Stella. 'We found these hidden in your luggage. And a large dose dissolved in one of your bottles of gin. To get such a large amount of them, you would have to deal with illegal sources.'

53

'I've never seen them before!'

Ng looked at her blankly for an eon or two. Stella felt cold. A single drop of fear-sweat rolled past her ear and plopped on the floor.

A stick-figure female with horn-rimmed specs entered. She had a whiff of Olive Oyle, Popeye's love, about her. Stella's showbiz mind drifted – this lass would be perfect casting as the No Nonsense Virgin Cop in *The Homicide Boys*. The woman whispered briefly in Ng's ear, gave Stella a long hard look and left.

Stella had caught a couple of phrases. 'Morgue papers', and 'fingerprints'. So they must already be ripping the body open to see what's what.

'Thank you for your help, Miss Pentangeli.' Ng rose and escorted her to the door, as polite as any maitre d'.

'I didn't do it, Investigator, and I think you know that.'

'Why do you think you know that I know that?'

'There's an extra set of prints on the knife, isn't there?'

*

It was as though this maddening woman had written the interim report herself. If this Stella Pentangeli was innocent, she was good. If she was guilty she was very good. Or very very bad.

Ng didn't confirm or deny the existence of the extra prints nor tell her whose extra prints they were. Jeddah Magnum's.

8.

666

Nelson knelt on the grass in Bush Creek Forest, hidden from Faust Hall praying to his God. After his bashing at the hands of drug dealers and his subsequent epiphany, he'd fallen gratefully into the hands of YHWH and committed his life to Him.

He had no clear image of YHWH but he knew what He wanted. That night in the alley, YHWH had upbraided him for his moral failings and rotten life so far, chastened him for his pride, humbled him totally. YHWH spoke thus: *Pride makes men turn their backs on the Most High and think they can just sail along merrily through this vale of tears and not pay a price for their detours and false trails. You, Nelson, have come too far too quick too cheaply. You got too much too soon too long. You got too big for your britches, too smart for your own good and it's time to fork over some dues.*

As if with a whip of scorpions YHWH had pursued Nelson, and so transfigured and transfixed had Nelson been that he returned a few nights later to pay homage in the alley, his road to Damascus. By chance, the three young muggers were back again, waiting for a new victim and – lo! – it was victim #1! Unable to believe their luck, they set upon him again.

But this time born-again Nelson, who had never been a fighter, slew them good. The Lord had placed on the ground — in lieu of the jawbone of an ass — a length of stout lumber. Its height was four inches and its breadth was two inches and its length was that of an arm.

Nelson had picked up the stick and smashed it into the first youth's face, breaking his nose and making him cry. The other kids tried to run, but Nelson had grown wings. He broke the stick upon them then picked up a brick and smashed them further till they fled.

Nelson's new invincibility extended to his cold turkey. He hadn't suffered the slightest in withdrawing from the smack, or the mboké, or the toot, or the hooch. YHWH saw to it that he sobered up and became His soldier just like that.

*

On this day the Lord had made, under this tree the Lord had tinged with green and kissed with dew, scarcely a quarter mile from Faust Hall and its sorrows and sinners and torments, Nelson gave thanks for his deliverance. He had been to The Fortnight twice before, when he'd been a name, and oh how he'd sinned in those Godless days. He drew a discreet veil round the memories and thanked YHWH that this time it was different. He was a stranger in a strange land, and they were strangers to him. They were as lice on Lucifer's back.

As he was praying, he heard a noise from a patch of bush. Ever since the night he'd met YHWH he no longer feared such noises — in fact he welcomed them. The Lord had shown him he had the power of ten men and he rather looked forward to some activity in the biff department.

Nelson stepped forward bravely — and found himself looking into the eyes of a monstrous being. The eyes were wild and red, the skin was blistered and yellow, the hair was spiked and spreading up and out from the scalp as though this creature had been caught in a lightning storm at the beginning of time.

'Are you real?' asked Nelson.

The vision just stared.

Nelson, beyond reason, stared back. He saw – lo! – that the being had only nine fingers.

Turn 9 upside down and it's 6!

3 times 6 is 18! 1. 8.

1 plus 8 is 9!

999!

666! The number of The Beast!

Satan was here!

Nelson screamed in terror. Instead of running to Faust Hall, he ran further into the forest. The tiny part of his mind that was still sane knew that this was a dumb move but he seldom listened to the sane bit any more.

9.

heartless actors

Specialist Probationary Constable Pauline Playne figured Jeddah Magnum had to be the prime suspect.

Magnum was a grossly overweight loser who lived in some pissy caravan park all year except for two weeks when she got to meet all the grand people who, unlike her, had succeeded in showbiz—and Client Google was one of the biggest successes.

It was Magnum's knife in Google's heart. Under the pork, Playne suspected, Magnum had the muscle to slip the knife in. Also, she was tall enough.

She had a master key to all the rooms.

Ng wasn't so sure. 'So her motive is what, jealousy of Client Google's triumphs?'

Playne bored in. 'Google was the sort of arsehole who'd carry a few grand in his pocket to impress women. Magnum could use that sort of money.'

Ng looked at SPC Playne. His face gave away nothing, but he was thinking she might just turn out to be a good investigator. 'Let me ponder it, Constable.'

Playne beamed. Making any sort of impression on Ng's thinking was the MVC&IP equivalent of a knighthood.

*

Stella wrote it like a stranger, as if she'd cry if she got too close to it.

SHOWBIZ! SHOWBIZ! SHOWBIZ! ONLINE!
THE PENTANGELI PAPERS *EXCLUSIVE*
MURDER AT THE FORTNIGHT! DEVELOPING STORY!
The corpse of notorious nabob TV exec from hell Lou Google was
found this morning in a bed in student digs at glam Gothic Faust
Hall in bucolic Bushy Creek presently hosting this year's
The Fortnight. Jilted writer? Insulted actor? Rival Network
Programmer? (Take your prick.) The lady showbiz detective is on
the job. As showbitch aficionados know, Lou was just about the
heaviest hitter in network TV and . . .

It was a eulogy Lou would have enjoyed had it not required him to die so violently in order to get it. His career highlights, his brass balls, his courage in clambering to the top were all noted and applauded.

Stella was glad they'd, so to speak, 'made up' just before he died. She finished her 600-word piece in the dining hall on her trusty laptop, then emailed it to Terry to format and post.

Now, in her new room away from the crime event bedroom, events finally caught up with her. She sobbed like a broken woman for a man she'd hated who'd died violently as she slept next to him, and she wept for the guilt she felt at the joy it was him who was dead and not her.

*

When she was agitated, Jeddah had a habit of not so much smoking her cigarettes as inhaling them whole—a train smoker. She'd done four newspaper interviews and two radios by phone before Investigator Ng threatened to arrest her for hindering the investigation. He left a fuzzy-cheeked local uniform to mind her and the boy was always there, staring at her like some kind of village idiot gazing at a particularly interesting cow.

She sat beside the window in her tiny temporary office – it overflowed with posters, books, schedules and scripts – and blew smoke out of her lungs like a smoky whale. Jeddah needed The Fortnight to continue or she'd be out at least fifteen grand and she'd be filing for bankruptcy.

She would *not* let The Fortnight go under. Put that in your ledger and underline it! Not today, not this year, not ever! The Fortnight was once, nearly, part of the world circuit of writers' conferences. To be part of that circuit would be . . . everything.

This Investigator Ng character seemed to have all the power and he'd be the one to convince. She rehearsed in her mind why The Fortnight should continue:

a) the show must go on

b) Lou would have wanted it that way

c) . . .

Ng surprised her by knocking politely on her door. 'Miss Magnum.'

'Investigator, we have an old saying in showbusiness – the show must go on.'

'I agree. I think you should keep The Fortnight open.'

'Lou would have . . .' She stopped in surprise, realising that she had won. Their faceless face-off was interrupted by a strange sound from the bowels of Faust.

Singing

Singing?

With a dead guest only just butchered like a hog? With the press baying for more story, more story? With her future in danger of sliding down the toilet?

Singing?

Who the fuck was singing at a time like this?

*

Fifty or so people had gathered by instinct in the bar. No one wanted to be alone in their cubicles or their heads right then. Many had felt the need for a stiff brandy.

'In view of the circ . . .'

'I usually never drink before . . .'

'I knew Lou and he was a . . .'

'Cheers. Glad he's dead if you want the truth . . .'

'Of *course* Stella did it . . .'

At the piano, Lucy Sky seized the moment. She started up what she thought was an appropriate song for a mourning morning – a sad bluesy number she'd recently composed.

> *Pull up the shade*
> *let some light in the room*
> *open the window too.*
> *Shake up the mattress*
> *straighten the bed.*
> *It's over.*

Her voice was low and strong – Aretha without tricks. Lucy was ripe and curvy but she was a teen for all that and the sound of this amazing voice, this womanly voice, this black voice coming out of a young white girl drew eyes and ears to her. The room became a pack of Norman Maines digging Esther Blodgett.

> *Make me some tea*
> *drink it down slow*
> *pretend I'm drinking for two.*
> *Shower real slow*
> *let the water flow.*
> *It's over.*

Death scared the Fortnighters and the death of a youngish tribe member scared them most. Lucy's song (and the booze) gave them back some of their courage – the courage that allowed them to dream a dream of being different and making it happen, that sent them into showbiz knowing the good odds that they'd end up old and broke and forgotten with a book of yellow clippings.

> *He wasn't much of a man*
> *but he was all right*
> *He made me comfortable*
> *ev'ry night.*
> *He wasn't much of a man*
> *but he was okay.*
> *I wish he was with me*
> *today.*

*

Jeddah burst in fully ready to chastise and upbraid. It was a mourning song but it was still a bunch of actors singing in a bar. She spotted two – no, three – journos mingling unobtrusively, their elbows protecting their open shoulder-bags where, no doubt, hidden cameras were filming. ('Tonight On *Night Night*! Heartless actors make whoopee over the body of one of their own!') The part of her that made her so good at her job took over the mouth before the brain had processed the words. 'Quiet please! Quiet please everyone!'

Lucy scowled and stopped. The journos tried to look invisible. The room came to a halt.

'Ladies and gentlemen, a toast to Lou Google.'

'Lou! To Lou.'

'Rest in peace.'

'Hear hear.'

While the bar was still a captive of Jeddah's organised decorum, the wily handmaiden quietly closed the bar room door and lowered her voice. 'I'd like to welcome members of the media here.' She singled out the two TV girls and the one guy – 'Derek, Deb, Debbi' – then, in a whisper, made the whole room a partner to her conspiracy. 'Anyone who knew Lou might like to team up with Derek Deb or Debbi to do a quick interview.'

The journos nodded their appreciation and quickly corralled a handful of famous faces in separate corners of the bar, where they could record their unbridled sorrow for posterity. Derek, Deb, Debbi knew what Jeddah was doing. In exchange for not airing footage of boozy, warbling Fortnight folk, they would be instead be beaming solemn, tearstained epitaphs from famous Fortnight folk battling their grief. And it would travel round the world. Or so Jeddah hoped.

Only one of the journos – Deb, not Debbi – got a sound bite from Lucy. Later, she was commended for her foresight. It turned out the camera loved Lucy's face even more than life did. Deb's current affairs show – *Hard Currently* – ran all 45 seconds of it, billing her as Lucy Sky, singer and actor and close friend of Lou, and concentrating as much as delicacy allowed on her breasts. If Lucy became famous, then *Hard Currently* would own the very first footage of her.

A near PR disaster. Jeddah had staved off ruin for another day. Just maybe, The Fortnight was on its way to being on the world map along with the New York Writer's Camp and The Paris Workshop.

Assuming, of course, no one else died.

10.

if you go down to the
woods today

Present in the room are Specialist Probationary Constable Playne, P.L.A.Y.N.E, Investigator Ng, N.G., and Miss Jeddah Magnum, M.A.G.N.U.M. I am recording this on a MiniCam 3000 with time and date clearly stamped. Copies of this tape will be supplied on valid request.'

'Now *that's* good dialogue, Investigator,' said Jeddah, all smiles. 'Can I steal it for one of my playwrights?'

Ng's return smile didn't reach his eyes. 'There is a problem, Miss Magnum, we ...'

'Call me *Jeddah*, please. Or I won't know who you're *talking to*.'

Jesus, thought Pauline, give it a rest.

Ng's smile stayed fixed. 'There is a murder weapon – a knife – and your prints are on it.'

'It's my knife, Investigator. So of *course*, my fingerprints are on it. I *told* the commander chappie it was my knife.'

'You told the local police?'

'Of course. First thing.'

Pauline and Ng exchanged glances. Ng nodded at Pauline, who strode out of the room.

'There's another problem. The master key.'

'What of it?'

'It's my understanding that during The Fortnight you are issued with the key so you can access rooms in emergencies.'

'Correctomundo.'

'With that master key you could have entered Miss Pentangeli's room the night Mr Google was murdered. You could have slipped TranQuax into Miss Pentangeli's gin bottle to make sure they'd both be out cold when you stabbed him.'

Around this time suspects usually start getting angry. Not Suspect Magnum. She trilled a delighted laugh. 'My master key's irrelevant, Investigator. I hear on the GV Stella's door was left unlocked.'

'GV?' asked Ng.

'Grape vine. As for killing Lou, he was, for all his faults, a supporter and friend of my Fortnight. One day it's going to rival the New York Writer's Conference and all the majors.'

Pauline re-entered and whispered in Ng's ear. 'It's true, sir. She told the local cops it was her knife in Google.'

Miss Magnum was a poor suspect. This death at The Fortnight would be the death of The Fortnight.

Ng was very naïve about things showbiz.

*

Like *tout le Fortnight*, Stella had been conscientiously avoiding Nelson. Showbiz people know that – contrary to medical opinion – madness is as contagious as failure. Whatever Nelson had caught as he slid down the helter-skelter they didn't want any part of. Only the kindest of them could listen to him talk about YHWH and Armageddon for more than a minute without begging him to shut the fuck up and take his medication.

So Stella was more than startled when Nelson emerged from Bushy Creek Forest screaming. He spotted Stella sitting on the lawn and ran towards her.

Oh shit!

She eyed a hefty stick near her feet that, she guessed, she could use as a weapon, but her knees, like her bowels, were water. Nelson ran right up to her face and yelled into it, 'I saw the Devil!' He sounded not so much homicidal as terrified and in need of help. 'He had nine fingers!'

Think fast! 'You saw the *devil?*' said Stella, all sympathy. 'You poor boy!'

'Run!'

'You run. I'll fight the devil.'

Nelson looked awestruck. 'You can *do* that? Fight the *devil?*'

'Sure.'

'Thank you, thank you.' He kissed her hand like a penitent sinner and fled towards Faust Hall.

Stella felt her heart rate sink back to ten thousand. *Nelson's sure nuts enough to be on the suspect list.* She was about to sit back down when it struck her . . .

Nine fingers? Robbie George had nine fingers. But he wasn't anywhere near Bushy Creek. Was he? Robbie was back in the city. Wasn't he? He was drunk in his pub. Although if Robbie *were* here, the contest for prime suspect would be a two-horse race between him and Nelson J. Christ.

Are there any sane people left in showbiz?

Stella was a city gal. She thought mankind was right to tame nature. She liked pavement under her feet and neon to light the way. On the few occasions when she'd looked up into a clear night sky, the sight of so many millions of cold worlds shining their dead light made her want to panic.

So it was rather brave of Stella to decide to go into the forest to see the devil. She considered enlisting Ng and the skinny Constable's help but her pride stopped her. She was the showbiz detective! She picked up a big stick.

*

Stella's skin was cold under the thick layer of trees. The forest was dark and spooky. Even this close to Faust Hall and civilization, there was a smell of decay and rot. It was a different world — green black and dangerous — and if the devil liked dank, this was a great spot to hang out.

CRACK! One loud burst of thunder. Stella jumped. Suddenly it was darker and a thousand tiny feet were heading her way. *Oh God! Rats!* But it wasn't rats. It was rain on the canopy of leaves. In the real word rain belted down. In the forest, it had just started trickling through to the earth.

'Bravo.'

Even as Stella's bowels were liquefying, even as she leapt in the air, even as her heart exploded in her throat, she managed to spin her head around and raise her big stick.

It was Ng, carrying a large and sensible umbrella.

'Come shelter under this, Miss Pentangeli. I hope I didn't startle you.'

Stella thought of forty or fifty replies and settled for: 'Thank you.'

She stood under Ng's umbrella and noted, amused, that he was so short he had to stretch his umbrella arm to full extension to accommodate her.

'Nelson said the Devil's hiding in here.'

Ng: 'I heard.'

'He said Satan had nine fingers.'

Ng: 'I know. Like Mr George, the playwright.'

'You know Robbie?'

Ng shrugged modestly and Stella guessed this character knew a lot of things and wouldn't be volunteering any of them easily.

'Robbie couldn't be here. He's — '

Ng: 'I know.'

She hated Ng, she decided. On top of his cop versus civilian

67

superiority, there was his man versus woman superiority and on top of *that*, he probably carried oriental versus round-eye baggage too.

'Shall we go?'

They headed for Faust across soggy ground.

*

The music room was the field office and Pauline had set it up well, scrounging extra whiteboards and a desk. Before allowing Stella in, Ng excused himself to place a blanket over the main whiteboards.

'Is Mr Sharp all right, Constable?'

'For a lunatic, I guess so, sir. Local uniforms have locked him in a food pantry.'

'Bring him here, would you please?'

Pauline headed off. Only then did Ng let Stella in the room. He sat her down. 'I'd like you to help me, Miss Pentangeli. To consult with us on the case.'

Long surprised pause from Stella, then: 'Me? Why?'

'My superiors think you can help.'

'They do? Do *you* think I can help?'

Ng looked discomfited. 'I don't understand theatre people, Miss Pentangeli. They're like Martians.'

'I'm a Martian too.'

'You, at least, appear to have spent some time on earth.'

Stella burst out in a quick bray. This was the first time she had heard Ng venture a joke. His expressionless face, deadpan voice – even his timing – were perfect.

'Let me be frank, Miss Pentangeli. Just about everyone I've met here so far is a stranger to me. I need a guide, an interpreter. You're intelligent and brave and you want to clear up this event, this murder. You're perfect.'

'So I guess I'm innocent after all?'

He didn't quite answer the question but instead moved to his ultra-neat desk, found the fax he was looking for and waved it at her. 'Specialists' report on the knife in Client Google seems to clear you.'

'Can you do that in English?'

'City Specialists (Coroner Support) concludes the knife that killed Mr Google was introduced into the client's chest by someone taller and much stronger than you. Plus, with all those TranQuax in you, they doubt you could have functioned with sufficient skill.'

'Short, weak, drugged-up and innocent, huh?' Stella couldn't tell whether Ng had even heard her. 'Did Lou have tranks in him too?'

Ng paused. She was, after all, a civilian. But – 'Yes he did. A larger dosage. Much larger.'

Stella's mouth went dry. 'That's why Lou was so easy to kill! He was out like a rock! But, Lou *never* took drugs. He only kept stuff around for seduction purposes. Had this thing about his body being the temple of his soul.'

'His blood refutes that. I'm going to interview Mr Sharp now. I'd like you to sit in that cupboard and . . .'

'Don't tell me. Eavesdrop.'

'Well, yes.'

'Like a rat.' Before he could rephrase, Stella went on. 'Okay. I'll sit in on Nelson's interview. But not in the cupboard. I'm not a rat, Investigator.'

'You're not a police either.'

'Consultants don't sit in cupboards.'

Ng gave in, as he'd planned from the start. 'I have to tape the interview.'

'I know.'

'I have to have another police person present.'

'I know.'

Ng looked at Stella stonefaced and went to the door where the sour Pauline was just arriving with Nelson.

'Come in now, Constable. Mr Sharp, please.'

Pauline entered with Nelson, closed the door, and sat him down.

'Present in the room are Consultant Stella Pentangeli P.E.N.T.A.N.G.E.L.I., Specialist Probationary Constable Playne, P.L.A.Y.N.E, Investigator Ng, N.G., and Nelson Sharp, S.H.A.R.P. I am recording this on a MiniCam 3000 with time and date clearly stamped. Copies of this tape will be supplied on valid request. Now Mr Sharp, how are you feeling?'

'Humble the proud.'

'That's a fine motto.'

'Slaughter the mighty!'

'Well, as a policeman, I don't like that motto very much.'

Stella, Playne and Ng all chuckled but Nelson wasn't buying their fakery.

'Did you kill Mr Google last night?'

No response from Nelson.

'Did the devil kill Mr Google?'

No response.

'Has the demon with nine fingers reappeared?'

No response. Nelson had migrated to Venus or Alpha Centauri.

'Mr Sharp,' said Ng. 'You need medical help. We are going to see that you get it.'

Nelson stared.

'Constable, escort Mr Sharp out, please.'

Pauline opened the door and led Nelson away. Stella's mouth went dry. She closed her eyes and concentrated. She smelt it. Perfume. She'd smelt it first – when? – first night – which? – first night of the State Theatre production of *Bar*

Code Blues. Who? Cordelia Heath. They'd passed – ships in the night – in many theatre foyers and nodded briefly.

Stella moved to the door and there she was. 'I thought I smelt your perfume, Cordelia.'

'It's not perfume,' Cordelia informed Stella in her low, trained-actor voice. 'It's herbal water.'

Ng joined them. 'Surely you were not spying, Miss Heath.'

'Certainly not.'

Ng smiled. 'Of course not, how silly. Now that you're here, come in, please.'

Cordelia had the look of a wilful adolescent determined not to be bullied by the grown-ups. Even though she towered over Ng, he guessed she was one of those people so fearful of authority they go out of their way to defy it to prove they aren't fearful.

'Present in the room are Specialist Probationary Constable Playne, P.L.A.Y.N.E., Investigator Ng. N.G., Miss Stella Pentangeli, P.E.N.T.A.G.E.L.I., and Miss Cordelia Heath. H.E.A.T.H. I am recording this on a MiniCam 3000 with time and date clearly stamped. Copies of this tape will be supplied on valid request. Now, is Mr George here at Faust Hall, Miss Heath?'

Cordelia frowned, puzzled at the stupid question.

'Not that I know.'

'In the forest, perhaps?'

She laughed briefly. 'The only "forest" Robbie would be in is the local park with the other winos.'

'Mr Sharp saw a nine-fingered man – creature – in the forest.'

'Mr Sharp is insane.'

'If Mr George is in the forest, Miss Heath, you'd best tell me now or you'll be charged with hindering an investigation. If he's involved in this event, you'll face an accessory charge.'

Brrzztttt! It was the wrong choice. Cordelia clammed up, a martyr to the cause of Fuck Tha Police.

'Cordelia,' said Stella, 'Robbie might have killed Lou.'

'I didn't realise you'd joined the force, Stella.'

'Miss Pentangeli is being of invaluable service to me.'

Smirk. 'I bet she is.'

Ng: 'Thank you Miss Heath. Sorry to trouble you.'

'Yeah.'

Cordelia stood, stalked off, haunch first. She was magnificent. Even Ng couldn't keep his eyes off the haunch.

*

All the way from Bushy Creek, Nelson tried to explain to the two impassive uniform cops why they should stop the car and release him right now! YHWH needed him. He'd sent him to The Fortnight for a reason.

'Yeah. To stab some poor prick in his sleep.'

Nelson ignored the calumny. 'There was an angel of the Lord in the forest – or it could have been a demon. Anyway the visitation tried to warn me but I, unworthy coward, fled!'

'Will you shut up?'

'The time of tribulation has come, fellas! The End of Days is The End of The Fortnight! Don't you *get it?*'

'*Shut up!*'

'The Fortnight is fourteen days! That means the End of Days is going to be *fourteen times* as bad!'

The uniforms looked at each other as Nelson babbled on. This ride was gonna be one to tell the wife and kids.

*

The emergency entrance of any major mental hospital is usually disappointingly quiet. While the urban myth that more people go nuts at full moon is actually true, even at peak hour there is no stream of ambulances and police cars and irate relatives flooding the place with ravers and psychos, gibberers, Jesuses, Napoleons, alien inductees and abductees, with brides of Frankenstein and angries with tinfoil hats to ward off the CIA's thought control rays. In these halcyon Prozac years, things are calmer, more processed, smooth.

Which is what someone forgot to tell Nelson.

Perhaps if the uniforms and the male attending nurse at City Mental had been aware that Nelson had so easily smitten three strong young drug thugs they would not have been so cavalier. Or perhaps they would. Any country cop who thinks he can't take down one skinny *actor*, for Chrissakes, ought to reconsider his employment status. And any male attending nurse of appreciable height, weight and strength who thinks he can't subdue anyone anytime anywhere with or without the help of a couple of country cops – well, such attending nurses don't exist.

Against all the rules, cop #1 left the keys in the ignition as he went to help nurse and cop #2 escort the now almost catatonically subdued Nelson into the hospital.

Again, against all the rules, when Nelson softly complained that his handcuffs were too tight, they opted to loosen them only metres from the main self-locking door. The rules state – and this was very firmly pointed out in the Mental Health Commission's findings – that the prisoner remains in police custody until restrained or incarcerated by the receiving authority and a receipt signed to that effect. So it was officially #1 and #2's fault that when Nelson's right hand came free of the cuffs, he pounced on them like a roaring lion.

He kneed #1 in the groin – OAF! – and that was the end of #1 until he awoke three hours later in the nut house infirmary.

An elbow to #2's throat – THOUCK! – cut off his air and slowed him down long enough to give the still supremely self-confident nurse a chance to swing his hairy fist at Nelson's head and connect squarely on the side of it. THWUNK! A blow like that was normally sufficient to bring any client to his senses or, better, to senselessness but Nelson shook off the blow like a pesky mosquito and head-butted the nurse – WHOCK! – blinding him with blood and pain.

As though born to war, Nelson shoved the squealing nurse over the prostrate form of #1 and, tripping, the nurse crashed into #2, whose larynx was now so swollen he was in danger of suffocation. For some panicky reason, #2 started to pummel the nurse, who started to pummel back.

The Mental Health Commission was invited to reach the conclusion that one or more City Mental nurses could and should have rushed from the building to intervene but instead waited, cowed, inside, fearful of the one-man killing machine who was dismantling any and every authority figure in sight. Counsel for the hospital and the Nurses Association, however, pointed out that the fracas lasted no more than ten seconds and a scant few seconds later Mr Sharp was behind the wheel of the police car and hurtling through the gateless main gates of City Mental.

*

The police car was found five hours later, abandoned in an underground car park. Though it was not reported in the media, a large, well-formed, remarkably healthy stool was found on the front seat, courtesy of Nelson's bowels. It was never established whether this was a deliberate insult from the prophet of YHWH to the powers of Babylon or if he'd been genuinely caught short.

Investigator Ng was not happy to learn that Nelson was on the prowl again. Not when the last pronouncement Nelson had been heard to utter was that Armageddon was coming to Bushy Creek and he wanted to be there.

11.

légion d'honneur

While Nelson was being escorted to the nuthouse, Ng, Pauline and the newly christened Consultant huddled.

'What did you think of Mr Sharp? Speak freely, Constable. Miss Pentangeli has my full confidence.'

'Pauline.'

For a second, Stella thought she was using some piece of arcane cop argot.

'Pauline Playne.'

Stella realised she was introducing herself.

'Stella.'

Ng: 'Anyone want to go first?'

Pauline launched: 'Mr Sharp could have done the client. But if he did see someone in the forest, that someone could also have done him.'

Investigator Ng turned to Stella. 'Mr Sharp said he went to the forest to pray. Does that sound reasonable?'

Stella was being invited in and Ng was telling Pauline that he was inviting her in. Stella felt a sense of calm. Her mind was clear. 'Nelson was never violent,' Stella said carefully, 'even when he was quote unquote famous.'

'He beat up those young druggies,' Ng pointed out reasonably.

'With a two-be-four hunk of lumber and a brick,' added Pauline. 'God told him to.' They ignored her.

Ng pondered. 'The problem is, the scene of Client Google's event was very tidy.'

'So?' Pauline and Stella in stereo.

'So we know Mr Sharp is capable of violence and mentally unsound. If he's to go berserk and do Client Google, would he leave such a pristine scene? And why not do the client's companion too?'

'He means me,' Stella said to Pauline, who nodded, I know.

'Anyway, let's give him Suspect status.'

'Not Prime Suspect?'

'Not yet. Move on.'

'Are we ruling out Jeddah Magnum?'

Stella: 'Why would Jeddah kill Lou?'

Pauline shrugged. 'Lust. Jealousy of you. Psychotic episode. Fun.'

'There's a big problem with Miss Magnum's motive,' said Ng.

'What's that?' asked Stella.

'The bad publicity will kill her Fortnight stone dead.'

Stella looked at Ng incredulously. 'Are you kidding? You can't *buy* publicity like this!'

Ng and Pauline looked at her, appalled. These showbiz folk, they *are* from Mars.

Ng: 'Let's not rule her out.'

He stood suddenly and swept the blanket off the whiteboards. Pauline started to protest, but decided against it and Stella understood instantly. Ng was letting her into the case fully. This was an act of faith. It was like Ng was awarding her a Légion d'honneur.

On whiteboard #1, some photocopied snapshots were

blue-tacked next to neatly printed notes and dates. *Stella*, *Jeddah*, *Nelson*, *Robbie*. Ng moved the photo of Nelson to whiteboard #2, on which was printed *MIN SUS*, *SUS*, *PRI SUS*, standing for – Stella wisely guessed – Minor Suspect, Suspect, Prime Suspect. Nelson and Jeddah were each Sus.

'I'm only a Min Sus?' she said, pretending irritation.

Constable Playne spoke up. 'No forensic. You're either a criminal mastermind or innocent.'

The whiteboards told Stella at a glance that the investigation was in trouble. The Nelson photo was a publicity still Stella recognised from *The Young and the Naked*. He'd been pretty then – now he was a bug-eyed loony. Stella's own mug shot was an enlarged copy of her old newspaper column masthead. She looked young and grainy. Stella marvelled at how quickly Ng had gathered the material together.

'What about Mr George?' said Ng, picking out Robbie's photo, which made him look a dangerous customer. Ng put the shot experimentally next to Nelson's.

Pauline jumped in. 'I fancy him. If he's anywhere round here, Mr George is capable of stabbing the client. Sober or in blackout.'

Getting the hang of it, Stella stuck her toe in the water. 'Don't forget, Robbie was sent to prison for armed robbery. He even fired a shotgun. And he used to beat up Cordelia Heath, his then wife.' She grinned, pleased with herself.

Ng had a dislike of imprecision. 'My understanding, Miss Pentangeli, is the shotgun he used in the robbery discharged accidentally and that he used violence on Miss Heath once.'

Stella flushed. He was right, but still. Robbie was Pri Sus.

'Then again, all this could be hot air and the doer was a local,' Pauline added wearily.

This was going to be a long session.

*

Hawkeye had arranged for Ng and Pauline to be accommodated at the Bushy Creek Hotel, but Ng had declined. He found Faust eminently suitable for a man of his monkish disposition and, far from 'contaminating the investigation', Ng suspected the closer he was to the scene, the sooner he'd find the truth.

He had asked Pauline to get a room next to his so they could more easily confer. She normally treated his whims as iron rules but the next day she'd asked if she could stay somewhere away from the action, perhaps on another floor.

Ng had agreed but he was surprised. Don't say she'd found a *boyfriend*? The Constable? *Here?*

12.

eros #2

Emu Gentle had to admit it. Lucy Sky was one hell of a
singer. Even a cappella, she sounded strong.

> *I know who I am*
> *I know what I is*
> *I'm black and I'm proud*
> *Mind your own biz (ness)*
> *I'm a B.L.A.C.K. man.*
> *Yeah.*
>
> *My mother was black*
> *My daddy was white*
> *He taught me to fear*
> *She taught me to fight.*
>
> *I'm a B.L.A.C.K. man.*
> *Yeah.*

They were sitting in the Faust garden under a fingernail moon
at the very table poor Lou had sat at the first, last and only day

he spent at this year's Fortnight. Emu had come out, he told himself, for a breath of fresh air.

'You sing great, you write great and you look great. You got a great future, girl,' he said.

Lucy shrugged prettily – 'Thank you' – but she had a million thoughts, all of them pushy.

'Emu,' she ventured, 'none of the "Midwinter" songs have melodies yet. Maybe I could write them. You could even maybe record them with me. Duet, like. It'd be great, don't you think? You've done everything else – film, TV, stage, activism, chess – why not a CD? What d'you think?'

What did he think! He'd just spent a couple of hours pouring shit all over the fucking play and now she wanted him to sing the songs? But God she was beautiful in her optimism and strength and, yes, her youth.

Lucy watched Emu watching her. God he was beautiful with his talent and his perfect features and ivory teeth.

Emu reached out and touched her face, his fingernails the same family of pink as her lips.

They stood together and instinctively moved out of the light. They kissed.

She reached down and touched his crotch. Gimmee.

He stroked her breast.

She lifted her top, needing to feel skin on skin.

Yeah.

*

Ng sat in solitude in the dark of his crib weighing up suspects. Miss Magnum was – so to speak – a slim possibility. Mr Sharp too.

Then there was Mr George. The local police had formed a search party with many an eager Bushy Creek citizen and combed the forest three miles either way and three miles in. Nothing.

'If this George character was here, he's long gone,' said the Commander.

Ng had nodded but didn't believe it for a second.

'Come on, Investigator, you don't believe that madman's story, do you?'

Well, yes. He did. Ng got a glass of water, downed it and thought some more.

At least The Fortnight had not broken up in panic and confusion. If that happened, Ng would be in trouble. He needed the doer here in Bushy Creek — not part of a Fortnight diaspora scattered across the country and around the world. He sipped his water and thought.

*

The needles of hot spray were almost painful on Stella's back as she turned up the pressure just a bit more. God, if she only had hot water like this in her home, she'd never leave the bathroom. The steam enveloped her. She could have been in the middle of an ocean fog a million miles from shore. She thought she heard the taps in the shower stall next door go into action and felt a weird kinship with whoever was sailing into their own ocean beside her.

THUD!

Stella realised there were two (three? four? more?) people in the cubicle next to her. She remembered how she'd wanted to shower with Lou Google just before realising he was dead. That thought creeped her out. Her thoughts turned to the shower scene in *Psycho*. It occurred to her that the knife in Lou's heart was just about identical to the one Tony Perkins had in that movie. *What the fuck am I doing? I'm in the shower at midnight in a strange place where people die!!*

THUD! CRASH!

For several panicky seconds she thought Tony Perkins

81

was going to crash through the dividing walls. *How safe is the lock?*

What were they doing in there?

What the hell am I doing in here?

All went silent. Stella mopped herself and hurried back to her room feeling for all the world like she was ten years old again and the boogie man was on her trail.

*

'You came,' said Pauline. 'I thought you'd forgotten me.'

Investigator Ng would have been surprised at Specialist Probationary Constable Pauline Playne's appearance, here in her lonely little room. For the prim, bespectacled No Nonsense Virgin Cop was quite a different kettle of woman this night. She had a red ribbon round her neck ('Take Me! I'm gift-wrapped!'), and her body was barely covered by a flimsy pink satin and lace nightgown. Her hair was brushed and mussed and wantonly splayed—as her legs would have been had the cheap Faust Hall beds been wider. Like in *The Boyfriend* or one of Lou Google's cornball *The Homicide Boys* eps, just the removal of Pauline's glasses and the loosening of her hair had transformed her into a sex kitten full of blood and good oils and ready to do the doona dance all night long.

Oh yeah.

13.

robbie

An hour past noon. Robbie had survived exactly 36 hours in the chilly wet forest with surprising ease.

The search party had come and gone. No problem. They hadn't even come close to finding him.

He'd laid low, melting into the Bushy Creek National Park like Tarzan. Robbie had been bred in wild country near the sea. His grandfather had taught him bushcraft skills and an ease with the outdoors. Strange he should end up infamous as a wild city man, a writer who'd come into full brief flower in a stone cell barely larger than a vertical grave. Strange he now called a cheerless stone room in a brick hotel his world when once he'd had all this.

A heavy duty sleeping bag and two flagons of Bloodspoor's port. That was all Robbie had needed and it was plenty to get the Faust job done. But now he had a problem. The port was gone and the familiar panic of not having booze at hand settled on him. The car was supposed to be here to whisk him back to the city. They'd have a new flagon. But where was the car? Look for the little lane. It leads to the highway. It's a secret. Look for a dark car, a Bentley. Listen for horn beeps. Two then one then one then two. Where was the car?

Beep. Beep. (pause) Beep. (pause) Beep. (pause) Beep. Beep.

Robbie's hands started shaking automatically, already tasting the Bloodspoor's he'd been promised. He tried to stop himself from running so he could grab the flagon and dive into it but by now his hands were shaking so much that he gave up on dignity and ran all the way.

*

Robbie peered in the window of the black car and thought, Oh shit! Yasser Fasser was waiting in the black car grinning up at him. Beneath the day and a half of grime and dirt and wind and exposure, Robbie's face went pale but he didn't even try to run. What was the point? If Yasser could find him here, he could find him anywhere.

Yasser Fasser was probably Arab. Or Russian. Or Mexican. Some said he was Romanian Gypsy. Who knew? Yasser didn't know – or if he did, he wasn't telling. What mattered to him was that the close-knit, tight-lipped crime clans knew him for what he was – a hard man, skilled in intimidation – and they all employed him for that talent. His face and hair were oily, his eyes dark and slippery, his hands surprisingly girlish for the pain they caused.

It was Fasser who had cut off Robbie's little finger.

'Robbie 'orge, 'et in. 'ood to see ya.' Yasser never pronounced his Gs – maybe he didn't want to, maybe he couldn't, maybe his original tongue didn't have them. Who knew with Yasser?

'Ya 'ot the money?'

'Money?'

'Nineteen thousand dollars.'

Robbie felt like he was in a time warp. He'd already had this conversation and it had ended up with him losing a finger. Of course he didn't have any money. Why would he have any money? He was broke when he went into the forest and he was just as broke now, and about to become very very thirsty.

Yasser laughed. 'Hop in.' He handed Robbie the Bloodspoor's, gunned the car and off they purred.

'Drink up, Robbie. We don't want our special 'uest 'oin into DTs. Ha ha ha. Ya be stayin with me a few days.'

It wasn't an invitation, but Robbie nodded agreement anyway and took a long drink. Bloodspoor's was back in his veins and heading for his brain at a rate of knots. Soon it would all be all right for a while.

14.

college of carnage

A few of the less kind Fortnighters thought Stella had done the deed on poor Lou, and that this Ng character (fabulous casting for offbeat cop) was stringing her along by getting her to 'assist' with the investigation to trap her.

'Stella Pentangeli is a detective like I'm a happily married man. She . . .'

'I heard from a friend in the police that Investigator Ng's gonna pull out the handcuffs any second now. She . . .'

'Don't you mean lady showbiz defective? Ha ha ha.'

Last night's triumph! conquest! *coup!* – 'Midwinter dreams of a dead black man' – had, however, succeeded in focusing minds back from murder to art. In the shiny clean dining hall, there was a happy buzz over campus-style eggs and bacon, sausage, tomato and cereal. A little bit of violent death seemed to cheer up everyone no end.

'I hope Emu and Stella didn't jump each other or Emu'll be next. He he.'

'I heard Stella and Cordelia were an item, Sappho-wise. They . . .'

'I hear movie rights for "Midwinter" are already on the table. Big bucks.'

'Ahhh!'

*

Later it seemed ridiculous to them that they could possibly have heard the cleaner's scream. She was, after all, on the second floor of the residential block. But it was loud and clear. 'Ahhh!'

The hall went real quiet real quick and a few of the braver souls got up and headed for the sound, then the rest followed.

'Ahhhh!'

There it was again.

The showbiz beast climbed the stairs, rounded the corner and tried to follow the braver few into the shower block but all most could do was jam, cram, crane and push in vain to get a look in. There were so many of them crushed into the stalls and the toilet area, they flowed out into the hall.

'It's The Gent!'

'He's dead.'

'Lemme outta . . .'

'Ahhhh!'

'Stop screaming!'

'Why's he screaming?'

'The Gent? Ahhhh!'

Screaming is infectious. Even some braver ones were screaming now and in a second the mood of the crowd changed and everyone screamed and wanted to go back, to get out, to move away, to flee wherever it was that was freaking people out in front.

The crowd turned and ran *en masse*.

87

*

As soon as Ng arrived he felt his heart sinking down the same shower stall drains as the excreted body fluids of the new client, who lay nude and dead on his back.

The crime scene was hopelessly compromised, of course. All those eager shoes, all those touchy fingers. Ng looked down at the body of Emu Gentle and knew that The Fortnight was finished. He scoped the stall, toilets and corridor with his MiniCam all the while praying Jeddah Magnum, room on the ground floor, or Robbie George, whereabouts unknown, or Nelson Sharp, whereabouts unknown, or Stella Pentangeli, room just down the hallway, had done it and was now willing to fess up to both murders.

Derek, Debbi and Deb thanked God they'd stayed around. None had been willing to chance leaving Bushy Creek until the other two did. *Tout le fortnight* thanked God they'd been spared and, as one, headed to their cubicles, stuffed their goodies in their bags, rushed for their cars and screamed out of the 'College of Carnage' (Derek) like surprised pagans who'd heard 'Judgement's Day's Last Act' (Deb) and 'Fled the Fortnight of Fear' (Debbi).

Ng didn't even try to stop them leaving. He scarcely even heard the engines revving and roaring off one by one and by twos and threes.

Those who knew the Investigator and thought him inscrutable, totally unruffable and even a tad cold-hearted would have been surprised at the weight of despair and panic that dropped into his soul right then. They'd have been flabbergasted to see tears well in his eyes as he looked at the sightless naked corpse of one of the few admirable people in this ridiculous menagerie.

*

The corridor was nearly empty now. Jeddah was there – the killer would have to slay her before she'd desert her post – along with Pauline, looking sticklike and sexless, and Stella, who moved up behind Ng. She had to tap him on the shoulder twice before he responded.

'I think I heard the murder,' she said.

Ng went on autopilot and barked orders at Pauline. 'Get that local doctor here. I need the client IDed and a time of death. Get the Specialists back from town. Get these reporters out of here. Miss Pentangeli, this way.'

Ng led Stella to the office. This time, he left the blankets over the whiteboards.

'I thought it was a couple having, you know, standing-up wet sex,' said Stella. 'In the shower. As one does sometimes. But thinking back, maybe it was the murderer murdering Emu. See, there was no talking, no laughing. A knee-trembler's worth a giggle or two.'

Ng knew he was blushing, knew Stella knew and knew she knew he knew. But he didn't say a word. He was truly, genuinely interested in hearing Miss Pentangeli explain why it was that the people around her – the men, anyway – just wouldn't stop dying.

'I know what you're trying to make yourself think, Mr Ng. I did it. I stabbed Lou, and liked it so much I went off and killed Emu. I know what else you're thinking. The media's coming after this story and if it's not solved quickly, they're going to eat you alive. And when they're done with you, they'll hand your bones to your boss. That's why you want it to be me or Jeddah or Robbie or Nelson.'

Ng, again, was unpleasantly surprised at how accurately she knew just where to rummage about in his head.

'By the way, does this mean I'm not a consultant anymore?'

*

There was something way way way at the back of Pauline Playne's mind as she worked the blood and fingernail crusties with her field equipment. From her time with Investigator Ng, she knew what he needed to know first and real quickly. Were there liquor or drugs in the client when he was done? If not, how the hell was a fit and strong young man overpowered so quietly and easily? The worrying thing popped up but was gone again before she could get a good look at whatever it was inside her that felt wrong.

As soon as she'd done the blood work – rough and ready but quick – she hurried into Ng's office, where she saw Stella looking suitably pale and harried.

Pauline whispered one word into Ng's ear. 'TranQuax.'

'Mr Gentle too?'

'Yeah.'

'Much?'

'Gentle was off his tree on them.'

'Enough to kill him?'

'No. But enough to make him killable.'

'Fingernails?'

'Not yet.'

'Go.'

'Yessir.'

She hurried from the room, the crusties already taking precedence over this deep worrying thing in her mind now going, going, gone.

*

Even if the distraught Lucy had a car, she would have been in no condition to drive. It was a three-hour train ride back to the city, so Cordelia took pity and offered her a lift, which Lucy accepted with humility. Since Lucy had caught a hasty glimpse of Emu's corpse most of her systems had crashed. Her motor functions were awry. Every now and again she found she hadn't breathed for a while and had to remind herself to start again. In. Out.

Lucy was at an age when nothing really truly bad had entered her life. She had suffered no irreparable, insupportable loss, had been shouldered with no burden that could have crushed her. But . . .

Death.

Was.

For.

Real.

She'd seen it in Emu's face. He was not coming back from where he was. He'd never smile again. He would be cut up by doctors and poked and prodded, then he'd be sewn back together and put in the ground, where his flesh would rot and things that eat rotted flesh would eat him, and these things would get hungry again and go looking for new meat, go looking for her.

Death.

Was.

For.

Real.

Could she stand the idea?

*

SHOWBIZ! SHOWBIZ! SHOWBIZ! ONLINE!
*THE PENTANGELI PAPERS *EXCLUSIVE**
ANOTHER MURDER AT THE FORTNIGHT!
EMU GENTLE! BRUTAL SLAYING!
For the first time in its 30-year history, among scenes of panic and fear, The Fortnight, one of the world's premier playwright's conferences, has been abandoned. It broke up this morning when the body of superstar actor and social activist Emu Gentle was found in a shower stall at exclusive residential college Faust Hall at Bushy Creek University. Gentle was, well, gentle but . . .

91

Stella filed a thousand words. Emu Gentle had often complained about white writers making black folks into saints and angels. But, try as she might, Stella's eulogy was a near-beatification of this wildly talented 'gentleman of the people'. She emailed the words to Terry Dear and opened a bottle of Beefeater, determined to relax herself into first sentimental mushiness, then indignation, then oblivion.

*

Cordelia's car was an ancient Volvo which rattled and wheezed. The sale of 'Midwinter dreams of a dead black man' would change all that.

She glanced at Lucy beside her and her heart went out. The mother she'd never found time or inclination to be wanted to pull the car over, wrap the poor kid in her arms and tell her that it was all right – no, not all right – tell her that death happened and it wasn't alright but it *was* part of the contract. No one gets out alive. We all have a shower stall in our future.

She didn't pull over, of course. After all, she and Lucy barely knew each other.

*

Cordelia dropped Lucy off at her family home in North Sweethurst. Lucy's mother took one look at her daughter and put her to bed, where Lucy fell asleep clutching a fluffy doll called Pookie, a childhood keepsake.

She clung to Pookie for dear life.

The next morning, her brother and sisters, none of whom could sing nor write nor play an instrument, were strangely respectful of her. The murders were huge and already Lucy's appearance on *Hard Currently* had attracted raves. She was a star! Plus some chick cop was coming to get her soon and she was going to be interviewed by The Homicide Boys about Emu Gentle the ex-superstar. Heavy.

*

In the forest outside Faust, it took Specialists Constable Playne and Investigator Ng a mere twenty minutes to find the six flagons of Bloodspoor's – famously, Robbie George's tipple of choice.

'You were right, sir. Mr George was here,' said Pauline Playne. 'The local cops seem to have graduated in Moron.'

Robbie George was elevated to Prime Suspect.

*

Stella's V-dub almost steered itself from Bushy Creek back to the city and – once it got the scent of home – galloped to her apartment at 6A Chatsbury Mansions. She was alive. She was home. Her apartment was neat as always – even sparse. Apart from books, she followed a golden rule – anything she hadn't used in six months, she threw out or gave to charity. Clothes, gadgets, even furniture. Anything. So her large two bedroom was neat and sparse and felt like Eden.

There the lamps for the indirect lighting she craved, there the TV, there the comfy guest couch, there her small but powerful DVD/cassette/turntable, there her music collection. Early Dylan. Early Stones. Beatles. Sex Pistols. Angela Drumm.

Stella loved the fact that she owned every brick and stick of 6A Chatsbury outright. She had determined, when her star still shone and her fees still glowed, that she would cease and desist from paying rent as soon as humanly possible.

Should it become necessary to sell up and hightail it out of town, she could escape with cash. Her beloved sanctum served a dual purpose. It was also her 'Fuck You' money.

93

15.

dream of the
handmaiden

On a hunch, Deb from *Hard Currently* had remained at Faust Hall after Derek and Debbie had left. She had her crew hide like thieves in the night.

Around midnight, they were treated to the bizarre and surprisingly rather beautiful sight of Jeddah The Hutt's Lady Macbeth Scene. She didn't seem drunk. She didn't seem stoned. She looked like she was sleepwalking, or in a trance. She was naked under dim corridor night lights, walking down the halls talking to herself weepy and sad. She'd touch a wall or a door or stroke a notice board like it was a lover's face, all the time muttering and laughing and chatting. Sometimes she'd go coquettish and she looked beautiful. The young Jeddah peeked out from the folds of face fat. Now and then she rested her forehead on the wall and closed her eyes and got lost remembering.

Only Deb knew what Jeddah was doing. She was grieving. She was saying farewell to the ghosts that haunted The Fortnight and her life.

Here was the spot where Willy Davidson had told her about the new play he had in mind. He'd finished it, too. It had gone to Broadway. Huge success. Made his name. Always said he owed it to Jeddah. Didn't you Will? Course you did.

Over here, Russell had wept when he told her he was going to Hollywood. You wanted it all, didn't you, darling? And you got it. Why so sad all these years? Cheer up!

And this was the site of the Battle of the Juliets, where not two but three women fought to the death over the pale and weedy body of an *enfant terrible* director who couldn't make up his mind which of the gals – all of whom he was screwing – to cast in his new rock and roll version of *Othello*. Oh Barry! Naughty!

And there.

And there.

God. And there! Up and down one corridor. Then up the stairs. Then again.

Finally Deb, tired of the sniggers and zooms and fat arse jokes, moved gently to Jeddah and led her unprotesting back to her room. Deb tucked her in and Jeddah, her face mottled with grief, seemed to fall asleep immediately.

Or maybe she was faking it so she could be alone.

Lou had to die, Jeddah realised. That was inevitable. It was the gods telling the world that drama and comedy and tragedy and farce were sacred. It was the gods saying you can't just put these holy things on a box and surround them with talking tomatoes and automobile ads and expect to escape retribution. Zap! Take that Lou Google! That was fate – justice, even.

But Emu?

The gods were slaughtering their sons now. The times were truly out of joint and Jeddah just didn't get it anymore. She put down the burden of sense. Let others pick it up and work it out.

Tomorrow, Jeddah would go back to her trailer in the Bushy Creek caravan park.

95

The dream of the handmaidens was over.
The dream of the handmaidens was dead.

*

Deb's crew were appalled when she asked them to destroy the
film of Jeddah's midnight stroll. They thought she was
kidding, saw she was not and refused. The camera crew naturally reported her to management – to the new Lou – who
thought about firing her but opted not to. Her gesture was
both cheap and expensive and, if it ever got out, would make
them the laughing stock of their peers. It was soft and stupid
and not at all in the best traditions of TV journalism, but
Deb was great at the job and this cheap sentimental streak
would fade.

part 2
i'm a no-good
murdering prick,
doo dah, doo dah.

Hawkeye

16.

i'm a no-good
murdering prick,
doo dah, doo dah

Years before, the very first female Commissioner of Police was called Constance Winters. Tradition now dictated that the current Commissioner – male or female – should be 'Connie'. Police Ministers were and had always been regarded as just fucking politicians who came and went. They were, every one of them – black, white, male, female, good guy, bad guy, left wing, right wing – known as 'Minnie'.

At the very start of his detective career, Ng got lucky. Official policy in the service changed to 'lateralism/specialistism' which, as far as anyone could figure out, meant loners like Ng were not only tolerated but held up as examples to be emulated. With the arrival of a new Minnie, a policy shift took effect – 'lateralism/specialistism' was bad. Individual initiative was all well and good but 'co-ordinated centralism with specialistism' was the wave of the future. This meant, as far as anyone could tell, that loners like Ng were now to be held up as examples of what modern cops should not be.

All this to-and-fro never even registered with Ng. His job was finding killers. He'd sacrificed his marriage on the altar of Investigator. Living people, it seemed, were not as strong as the pull of the hundred dead people he had avenged and the hundred more he would avenge.

Ng's weird work methods were protected by a succession of MVC&IP bosses because he was good – a clearance rate 10 per cent above-peer and 22 per cent above national average. Murder police are the crème de la crème, but even la crème must be team players/bureaucrats/record keepers. So, good as he was, Ng would have been out of the service years ago except for one other thing. He was a trophy.

'He's never in his MVC&IP *office* . . .'

'*So what?* He's got an office in his *head!*'

'He's an artist and his 409s and case notes are always perfect . . .'

'Do you want to tell the media our Asian trophy's got the boot?'

The last argument carried the most weight. The media – the TV and the net especially – loved Ng. Any Minnie or Connie who said, 'Say, fellows, we're firing Investigator Ng, our Asian trophy and best murder policeman, because he's a bit eccentric' might as well kiss their futures goodbye.

Early on, Ng decided, okay then, he'd be their trophy but they'd pay a price – they'll leave him alone to do his job his way.

*

Tuesday morning. Ng walked down the skinny halogen-lit corridors of One Police Towers into MVC&IP after a brief detour to Specialists (Central Forensics). Since co-ordinated centralism came in, the noisy open-space all-boys-and-girls-together had reverted to a series of tiny boxy offices. The IP part of MVC&IP was – and everyone knew it – a bad joke. Way back in the distant past it had been Internal Affairs, then the Police Integrity Unit, and it had been strictly segregated from and independent of the police service. The policio/

politico heavies gradually emasculated it and finally dumped it into the Murder and Violent Crimes basket where, as planned, it had languished and atrophied. *Quis custodiet ipsos custodes?* Who watches the watchmen? In this city's case, nobody much.

Ng's office – which he'd last entered a fortnight ago – had a half-jocular, half-not note pinned on the door. 'Missing Investigator! Have you seen this man?' There was a photo of Ng downloaded and upsized from the personnel files and a big blue arrow pointing at his head.

A couple of desultory investigative heads looked up as Ng headed for Hawkeye's office but no one bothered to wave or say hello. Ng knocked on the boss's door.

'Come!'

Ng entered. Hawkeye's office had a glorious view of the city which Ng knew the boss never looked at with either eye. They could have bricked it up and he wouldn't have noticed. The room was barely warm but the boss had his usual sweat stains on the armpits already.

'Good morn–'

'Two murders, Ng! Two events and no arrests! Two days! These are media corpses! Google was rich and heavy – TV! – and this Gentle character was a superstar! I been getting phone calls from round the world!' The boss sat back, feeling daring and vindicated. He'd often wondered what it would be like to tear Ng a new rectum. Now he knew. It felt great. He waited for Ng to talk so he could jump in again straight down his teeth. But Ng didn't talk and a full minute ticked by. Hawkeye tried again.

'Two days!'

Ng refused to bite.

'This is a Solve Or Die!'

Nothing.

'You ain't solving, Ng!'

101

Another minute went by.

'You got anything?'

'Yes sir, I do,' said Ng.

'Hard and stickies? Crusties?'

Ng put a small folder on the boss's desk. 'Two Bloodspoor's flagons found in the forest.'

'Prints?'

'No prints but it was cold. I suspect gloves.'

'Shit.'

'It's common knowledge in arts circles that the prison playwright and bank robber Robbie George drinks Bloodspoor's. Specialists (DNA, Seeds, Fibres, Assorted) matched dirt from the national park with the carpet in the Google bedroom scene. We have a sort of eyewitness who may put Mr George in the forest near the murders at the right time.'

'What do you mean a "sort of" eyewitness?'

Ng sighed. 'The problem, sir, is that the eyewitness – Mr Nelson Sharp – has a mental condition. He regularly talks to [consults notes] a deity he usually calls YHWH or I Am Who I Am. He doesn't claim he saw Mr George – he claims he saw Satan.'

'Satan, huh?'

'But Mr Sharp does insist the man or demon he saw had only nine fingers. Mr George had a finger forcibly amputated several years ago.'

'Was that the Mortaferi business?'

'Yes sir.'

For the first time, Hawkeye looked a little bit happy. 'But he saw a nine-fingered someone. And Robbie George has nine fingers? And this George also – very very unusually – drinks Bloodspoor's. *And* you found this stuff hidden – *hidden* – just a few hundred metres away from Faust Hall?'

'Yes sir.'

'And dirt from that very same forest was found in Google's room? Jesus, Ng! What more do you want? Do you want this George guy to start singing "I'm a no good murdering prick, doo dah, doo dah"?'

Ng looked at the boss in case he had another joke. Then: 'There's a small anomaly, sir. The same forest dirt was also found in a Miss Jeddah Magnum's room.'

'You think she might have done it?'

'No. But it was her knife that killed Client Google.'

'Robbie George could have stolen that knife, am I right?'

'Yes sir.'

'Jesus, Ng, you got hard and stickies on George for two murders. What's the prob?'

'I don't understand why Mr George would do these clients.'

'Who cares why? We got how, we got who. We got a doer.'

'*Possible* doer. Even *probable*. I'd like not to announce him Prime Suspect just yet.'

'Why the hell not?'

'He's gone underground. If we name him it'll drive him further underground.'

'We gotta tell Connie and Minnie something, Ng.'

'These are my events, sir. With respect.'

Respect. Right. Sure. 'I'll swear Minnie and Connie to silence.'

'They'll leak, sir. They always do.'

'But sometimes they hold their water for days, even weeks.'

'Yes sir.'

'How long before we can announce Mr George as Prime?'

'Give me a week.'

'You got three days.'

'Thank you.'

'No problem.'

'May I have Specialist Probationary Constable Playne officially seconded to me?'

'You mean "us" don't you, Ng? Seconded to "us" – seconded
to MVC&IP – seconded to the "murder unit".'

'Of course. That's what I meant sir.'

Yeah, right. 'No problem. I'll clear it with city area.'

'Thank you, sir.'

*

Lucy looked terrible. The greater part of her beauty was her
ripeness and energy and when they went – as they had for the
moment – she was just another teenager with scared eyes.

'Present in the room are Miss Lucy Sky S.K.Y., Specialist
Probationary Constable Playne P.L.A.Y.N.E, and Investigator
Ng N.G. Time is 8.40 am. Copies of this tape will be supplied
on valid request.'

With that out the way, Pauline sat back quietly to watch Ng
work on Lucy Sky, bimbo. She knew the power an interview
room had to inspire fear and – with luck – confession.

'Miss Sky, were you intimate with Mr Gentle the night he
was killed?'

'No.'

Pauline butted in. 'Of course you were. We have half
a dozen witnesses.' A lie, of course, but what the hey. If
Pauline Playne had her way, they would charge the little tart
with hindering police, lock her up for six hours and pretend
they'd lost her when the lawyers came looking. That'd rattle
her cage.

Ng played a hunch. 'You don't have to lie. The promise died
with him.'

Lucy looked at Ng sharply. How could he know?

Ng continued. 'You two made love. Love is good.

Immorality – sin, adultery – is not an issue here, Miss Sky. You were right about Mr Gentle. Your instincts were sound. He was worth chasing. So you flirted and chased and finally you had sex with him.' Lucy looked away. 'There in the garden. You just wanted him for a little while. A connection. A communion. To keep for memory's sake. After, he made you promise not to tell anyone – his wife, your friends, anybody. It made you angry.'

'I *was* angry.' She said it almost without realising.

'Lucy,' said Ng. 'All that matters is what happened in the shower cubicle around midnight. Did you bash Mr Gentle? Bash him until he died? Were you *that* angry?'

Tears sprang to Lucy's eyes. 'How could you think that? I could never kill him. He was my hero.'

The soft loving words of every stalker and celebrity slayer since Judas. I love him. I adore him. I'm his friend. I kiss his cheek. Take that. Bang.

'Tell me, Lucy.'

She didn't hesitate. 'Emu and I were in the garden for an hour or so. Finally I get him so horny, he lets me give him a BJ.'

'BJ?'

'Blow job.' Ng blushes and nods. 'He said it was only that or a hand job because he was faithful to his wife.' Nod. 'He was a real gentleman.' Nod. 'Then I went to my crib and crunched out.'

'Slept soundly,' Pauline volunteered.

'So you have no alibi for midnight?'

Fear filled her face. Whisper: 'No.'

'What about Mr Google? Did you have a BD or sex or whatever with him?'

'BJ. No.'

Given Client Google's track record with teenagers, Suspect Sky could easy have a motive to kill him too. In the privacy of his mind, Ng tried out the statement. 'Lucy Sky, I'm arresting you for the murders of Lou Google and Emu Gentle.' But it was wishful thinking. Ng looked inside and found he had absolutely no opinion about whether Lucy Sky was the doer.

17.

prophet

The *Pentangeli Papers*. Members' and visitors' comments. Monday 9.06 am.

Deer Penttangeli Papers – The jokes on you! I put them both to sleep then kiled them. Googel was a Jew. Gentel was a shitskin. Thus all members of the white Race will aveange.

*

As someone or other famously said about Los Angeles, there was no 'there' there. Thus it was with *The Pentangeli Papers*. There was Stella's laptop, there was Terry Dear's huge desktop computer in his mother's house and, every now and again, a meeting in The Sweethurst Caff, down the road from 6A Chatsbury. That was where *TPP* 'lived'.

The Caff, which Stella would normally have avoided on account of the showbiz types, had great coffee, so Stella put up with its starfucker ambience and autographed photos of movie 'stars'.

'Have an éclair, Terry, please.'

'No. I'm thin. I'm young. I'm a cyber-genius, Stella. *You* have an éclair.'

Stella liked Terry more than she could express. Terry was 19, gay, a cyber-resident who viewed the real world as merely a place to visit now and again to store up interesting facts to tell people online. As far as she knew, Terry was still a technical virgin although he'd had an online lover in Alaska for two years. They'd never met and probably, Terry said, never would. They were getting married online in a few months and Stella was to be maid of honour. She'd asked him a couple of times what exactly she was supposed to do at the wedding – did she go stand in front of his monitor? dial in? what? He told her twice but she didn't understand either time and stopped asking.

'The hits are through the roof. These murders at The Fortnight have been *great* for business.'

Then Terry looked at Stella with his 'don't bullshit me' face. 'So what were you doing in bed with Lou Google?'

'What do you mean?'

'I mean ... how come you and Google were doing the beastie?'

'It sort of just happened.'

'Stud-o-*rama*.'

'He drugged me with pantsdown pills, the son of a bitch.'

'Lucky tart. Stud sex *and* free drugs.'

'Terry!'

'Anyway. Congratulations. A couple of years without the jiggy-jig wasn't it?'

'A year and a half. Almost.'

'Ahhh!' Serious for a second. 'You okay?'

'Yeah.'

'Sure?'

'Let's talk *TPP*, huh?'

'The zine's flying. The readers love all that crime and murder shit. Arts-wise, Valerie and Rodney are at it again.'

Valerie and Rodney were stalwart subscribers to *The Pentangeli Papers*. They'd been having a cyber-war for months now about a modern dance piece called *Pee P.* in which the corps de ballet of the Birnberg Dance Company drank mineral water onstage and, for three hours, danced the roles of digestive organs as the water passed through their bodies culminating in a finale in which they urinated on the principal dancers. Valerie thought it was gross; Rodney, a masterpiece.

Stella wasn't listening. *The joke's on you. I put them both to sleep then kiled them. Googel was a Jew. Gentel was a shitskin. Thus all members of the white Race will aveange* – kept running round her mind. Terry had taken it down from *TPP* site quickly and thought nothing of it – some nutter – but Stella wondered how the poster had known both victims had been 'put to sleep, then kiled'. The TranQuax link hadn't been released to the media.

Terry was glaring at her. 'You didn't hear a word I said.'

But she didn't even hear that.

*

Ng was wondering about *The Pentangeli Papers* post, too. 'Deer'? 'Jew' is capitalised, 'white Race' and 'shitskin' aren't. Fluke? 'Aveange' – under-educated racist? Red herring? Ng didn't know. What he did know was it was emailed from an open access computer at Faust Hall yesterday morning around the same time as a cleaner was screaming in a shower stall over the body of a dead man.

*

Ng entered the Caff just as Terry was taking his leave.

'Miss Pentangeli.'

'Investigator Ng.'

'Wow! I saw you on *Hard Currently*!'

'Mr Ng, Terry Dear, my assistant.'

'How do you do?'

'Can you sign an autograph? The napkin's fine. Thanks! Bye Stells. Bye Investigator.' Exits.

'May I?' Sits. 'Is it convenient to talk here?'

'I'm not sure. Do I need a lawyer?'

Ng looked at her. She was one of those rare people whose face looked better when she was tired. Stronger. Determined. Chiselled. Constable Playne appeared even more skinny and haggard when she was fatigued. Miss Sky looked ugly, unreal, unfocused. This woman looked great.

'No lawyers. My superiors want your help again.'

'Don't schmooze a schmoozer, Investigator.'

'Very well. I want your help again.'

'Better. What do you want?'

'The "I killed them" post on your Pentangeli Papers site.'

Jesus! Stella thought. *He's monitoring my site.*

'You mean the "I kiled" single "l" post. Terry says it came from Bushy Creek yesterday morning.'

'We know. But we can't track who.'

Suddenly it seemed like every mobile in the Caff started bleeping at once and every manicured hand grabbed one.

'What?' said one denizen.

'You're shitting me,' said another.

'Cordelia Heath?' said a third.

There was a rush for the TV in the corner. Midday news. A demonstration outside Police HQ. Three hundred people gathered around a Thatcheresque Cordelia Heath. She's dressed in baggy proletarian black, one fist raised, megaphone in the other. She is mounted on the low stone wall outside HQ — always a good makeshift speaker's platform. There's the news crews. There's Deb. There's Debbi. There's Derek. *Hard Currently. North East West South. Night Night.*

'A great man was killed on Sunday night. A great black

man called Emu Gentle. And what are the police inside doing? Nothing!'

'Nothing,' echoes the crowd obediently.

'*What* are they doing?'

'NOTHING!'

Cordelia's fierce presence fills the screen and eats it up. It's a shame, thinks Stella, she hasn't done more soaps and dramas. The newsreader helpfully explains . . .

'spontaneous demonstration . . .'

'many of the country's leading actors, writers and directors . . .'

'Bushy Creek Celebrity Slayings'

Then Hawkeye appears and stands on the stone wall next to Cordelia. Back at the Caff, Ng mutters 'uh oh'. Hawkeye doesn't give good TV. His one glass eye stays locked in position while the other, nervous, darts around at his enemies. It makes him look like a demented pirate.

'I am in charge of all homicides in this state. My name is Unit Commander . . .' But the crowd is already booing.

'Get off! Let Cordelia speak!'

'There is a man we wish to contact . . .'

'BOO! Bullshit! Pull the other one!'

'Robert Murray George, aka Robbie George, the well-known playwright. We are urgently seeking his help with our enquiries.'

Great, thought Ng sourly. We didn't need Minnie or Connie to leak it to the media. Our own boss is quite capable, thank you. 'Help us with our enquiries'. Everyone knows that's as good as pointing a big red arrow at someone and saying, 'Look! That's the man! He's the murderer.'

Thanks to his moronic master, Ng's efforts to flush out Robbie's whereabouts were down the toilet.

The crowds at HQ and the Caff thrilled as the news sunk in.

111

Robbie George? Cordelia's ex-husband? Wow. Oh! the irony!
The tragedy! It's Shakespearian.

'We have an eyewitness!' Hawkeye continues, putting the
other size 13 boot in his mouth.

'Who?' asks Derek, Deb and/or Debbie.

Don't tell them, thinks Ng loyally. They'll crucify you.

'Nelson J. Sharp,' says Hawkeye.

'BOO! Rubbish!'

At the Caff, the patrons burst into laughter. Nelson J.
Sharp? The has-been religious maniac who's escaped from City
Mental – and who had done a big job on the seat of the police
car? He's the Commander's eyewitness?

'Get a grip you one-eyed wanker! BOO!'

But Fate isn't quite finished with Hawkeye yet. As though
sprung from hell itself, Nelson bounds onto the stone wall next
to a shocked Cordelia. The HQ and Caff crowds gasp. Deb,
Debbi and Derek's jaws drop. News crews go ballistic. An
insane fugitive from justice! Good stuff!

'Show business killed Emu and Lou Google both!' screams
Nelson, making a not-altogether unreasonable point.

Deb: 'Mr Sharp! Did you see the playwright Robbie George
in the forest at The Fortnight?'

Nelson stops and, for several seconds, the mad prophet
looks like what he is – a broken young man clutching at the
nearest salvation on offer. Did I see the writer in the forest?
Wasn't it Satan? Satan or guy? Satan. Guy. Satan. Guy.

'I saw *Satan*!'

Deb inches closer and shoves her mike right into Nelson's
face – which puts her much closer to the freak than Debbi or
Derek dared go. 'I want to get this straight, Nelson. You're
saying you didn't see Robbie George at The Fortnight?'

'I saw Beelzebub and his minions preparing for the End
of Days!'

Right about now Nelson goes down under the weight of six uniforms. The crowd boos. Cordelia screams 'Police brutality!'

Law and order, in the style of this city. And every glorious second of it captured live on international TV.

Hawkeye sees with hideous clarity that the eyewitness on whom he's staked the solution to these SODs is a crazy man who shits in cop cars. He thinks about it, then goes upstairs and writes out a request for early retirement. The Commissioner of Police accepts with alacrity.

18.

practical homicide
investigation

The dungeon was a gift to Yasser Fasser from a grateful Fuk Chin drugs chieftain. The wine cellar of an unremarkable suburban house had been outfitted with a steel door fitted by craftsmen. To avoid prying eyes a special entrance was added via the tiny back alley of Fasser's street. Guests – willing or not – could be spirited in and out without a soul knowing.

Yasser Fasser was not a kind man nor was he an intelligent man but he knew enough about police to know that the chances of Robbie being found in his dungeon were near zero – and that Robbie didn't seem to mind being there in the least. The dungeon had a state-of-the-art TV and Yasser had made sure to stock up on Bloodspoor's port.

Ex-cons, Yasser mused, are always less trouble. 'Used to 'ettin orders and bein' locked up, 'od bless 'em.'

This was not the first time Yasser had had a guest in his dungeon. In his line of work mini-kidnappings were a relatively benign alternative to killing. Locked away in sound-proofed calm, Robbie kept a disinterested yellow eye on the news of the search for him. He had no reason to doubt that Fasser was sincere when he told him, 'Don't worry. Ya be outta here three days, four tops. Is like holiday. Relax. Drink up.'

But if things went wrong, Robbie thought to himself, the same people who didn't know he was in this dungeon would equally not know in which shallow grave his corpse was hidden.

*

Pauline couldn't tell Ng of course. While plenty of police ended up in a love crib with suspects and even doers, they usually had the brains to wait until the case was closed, or to conduct their affair out of range of their colleagues.

Investigator Ng had a maxim which Pauline found useful. 'The answer,' he'd say, 'is in the question.'

Pauline had tried out Ng's maxim. Why did a lonely young heterosexual woman allow herself to be seduced by an intense and beautiful older woman? Which was the key word:

> lonely
>
> sexual
>
> seduced
>
> intense
>
> beautiful?

Pick an answer – any answer. Get Jung to help. Or Freud. Or Krafft-Ebing. And while you're at it, get them to tell me where I found the courage to ignore my upbringing and do the dyke rock. And with so little resistance!

Knock knock. I'm Cordelia. I brought some wine. Thought you'd be lonely.

Tick tock.

I want you.

I want you too.

*

A few weeks before, on the way to Bushy Creek with the Investigator, she had wondered aloud how Stella Pentangeli could have been so sluttish as to bed this Lou Google client within a couple of hours of seeing him for the first time in years.

The Investigator had remonstrated with her gently. 'When we're dead, the human heart is just muscle, Constable. While it beats, the heart knows the taste of the blood it needs.'

Pauline had been thrilled yet again by his wisdom and poetry, and her crush deepened even further. She had even daydreamed that he put a hand on her leg and suggested she pull over into a side road for a bit of sex. If he tried that now — i.e. after Cordelia — she'd wave him away scornfully. But she knew what he meant now. Her heart knew the taste of the blood it needed.

*

Cordelia insisted on absolute discretion. And what could be more discreet — and, for Pauline, more terrifying — than Lady Love, Sweethurst's cosiest lesbian bar. Dark. Romantic. Private. Pauline had never been inside a place like that, with real live lesbians. If you'd shown SPC Pauline Playne a flyblown corpse or a box full of spare hands in a hospital freezer, she wouldn't have flinched. She'd been present at an autopsy of a junkie who died when, desperate for a vein, she jabbed a syringe into her neck and straight into her spinal column.

Well, it took all that bravery and more for her to walk into Lady Love. And there was her Cordelia at the bar in her usual black. Pauline — a lifelong fan of the movie *The Killing of Sister George* — had dressed frilly and silly and girlie and lacy, which was much appreciated by some of the ladies who still clung to working-class overalls. Yummy. Dolly. Hi there.

Cordelia grabbed her and kissed her and Pauline melted once more.

The odds of Terry Dear being away from his computer *and* out of the house *and* in Lady Love were remote, but he was. Nor was there any reason Terry should have recognised the skinny chick swapping spit with Cordelia Heath, but he did. He'd compiled a *Pentangeli Papers* file on the major players in the Fortnight murders. Constable Playne was near the bottom.

'A *cop* playing tonsil tennis with a *witness?*' said Terry to himself. He rang Stella who was intrigued enough to ring Ng who told Stella not to worry, that he knew all about it.

Her mouth went dry. *He's lying.*

*

Stella had never tailed anyone before, and her criminology hand-books didn't devote any pages to it, so she cobbled together a few memories from TV shows and Sherlock Holmes novels. Blend in. Think grey.

She snuck her head inside the main door of Lady Love just in time to sneak it back out and run for cover. Cordelia and Pauline were heading her way. She pressed herself against the alley wall, feeling silly and excited all at once.

She heard the lovers exchange kisses and sweet words then watched them separate, Pauline walked down the street. Cordelia moved to her big old car, fired the engine and drove off.

Follow Cordelia. Stella's intuition advised.

Why?

Do it!

Stella's V-dub played catch up through the bohemian streets of Sweethurst, into pleasant well-to-do North Sweethurst and further into the not-so-pleasant, endless, numbingly alike suburbs. Cordelia's car came to a halt outside a non-descript brick veneer in Wuthering Park. Cordelia went inside. Now what? thought Stella. What if Cordelia has spotted her? Isn't this illegal? A dozen reasons tugged at Stella's sleeve and begged her to drive away right now but she didn't. She had talked the detective talk. Time to walk the walk. She got out of the V-dub, closed the door quietly and, trying to look like she belonged, headed for the quiet suburban house across the quiet suburban street in the quiet midnight moonlight.

She crept down the side of the house and found herself looking through a kitchen window at Cordelia and an Arab or somesuch.

'That's it. The whole nineteen thousand,' she heard Cordelia say.

''ood. The Doc will be 'lad.'

There was a wad of hundred dollar notes on the table. The Arab-ish man spotted her at his window.

'What the fuck?' she heard him say. As he headed for the back door, Stella headed for the street, her car and safety. As she ran, she fumbled for her car keys, rehearsing in her mind:

    1. fling door open
    2. shove key in
    3. turn it
    4. slam foot down.

Funnily, as she ran, she had time to think that she would have much preferred a few 'Stops!' or 'Come back heres!' from the man chasing her. She didn't like this professional silence. It meant he was saving his breath to run so he could get her.

1. fling door open!

That was as far as she got in her checklist. Yasser's tiny hands grabbed the back of her clothes, tearing them as he pulled her away from the car and towards him.

His hauled his right fist back to his shoulder, the better to crash it into Stella's face.

'No need for that, Mr Fasser.' It was said so quietly and clearly that Yasser's arm froze. And there was tiny Investigator Ng standing on the street looking for the entire world like a shy and apologetic next-door neighbour who hated to be a fusspot but wondered if they'd mind turning down the music.

"et outta here, pal. None of ya business.' Ng remained benignly silent so Fasser tried again. 'This bitch was spyin' on me.'

'Even so. I can't allow you to hurt her.'

"et outta here, pal, or I'll take care of you next.'

'Mr Fasser, it's me – Ng.'

Ng shrugged modestly – a gambler showing his winning hand to a guy who's been losing all his life.

'Mr Ng,' said Fasser sourly. "ood 'od. Didn't reco'nise you in the dark.' Stella saw Fasser's eyes flare as he calculated the odds. *Dare I do a cop? Dare I do Mr Ng?* It was a silly notion and the flare died.

Fasser let Stella go, and Sensei Kim Fat's ancient wisdom flooded back into her. 'Wherever you are, there is always something close at hand you can use as a weapon of self-defence.' *Streetfighting Techniques For Beginners.* Her right knee slammed upwards into Fasser's testes. 'Ki-ai!'

'Ahhhh! Holy shit!'

There was a subtle exchange of colours between hunter and prey. Stella's ashen face blossomed into a rich, angry, satisfied red while Yasser's dark face took on a green tinge.

Ng: 'Miss Pentangeli. Please.'

To Stella's eyes, Ng was acting the part of a gentleman appalled by such unseemly displays of violence. She heard him say: 'Miss Heath, hello.' Stella looked over Ng's shoulder and, sure enough, there was Cordelia in the night shadows. *How does he do it? He's a bat. He's Batman.*

*

Ng and Stella freed Robbie George from his dungeon. He seemed to accept his release with the same equanimity he'd accepted his imprisonment.

'I want to get you checked over at emergency,' said Ng.

'Nah thanks, Mr Ng,' said Robbie cheerily. 'I'm fine. Yasser's been feeding me really well.'

'Least I could do,' said Yasser through gritted testicles.

'He even insisted on getting me to bathe.'

'I even laundered his clothes,' Yasser said, proud of his (Jewish? Coptic? Romany?) hospitality to prisoners.

Yasser wanted an emergency doctor to examine his poor aching groin. But Ng said no and Yasser shut up about it. He didn't like the look in Ng's eyes.

*

Since the professional demise of Ng's one-eyed boss, MVC&IP was adrift and rudderless but still functioning after a fashion. Ng was, to all intents and purposes, untouchable unless the top links of the chain of command started rattling and made some decisions. Some of the more careerist murder unit police even deferred to him. Maybe he was acting boss. Who knew?

So when Ng walked into the unit's rooms with Yasser Fasser the multicultural enforcer, that dizzy bitch from the Reg Maundy *Rocky Horror Show* murder, that Amazon dyke who badmouthed the police this morning and Robbie George — well, everyone kept their heads down.

Ng put Robbie in interview room #1, Cordelia in #2, Yasser in #3. He put Stella in the shoebox they called his office.

*

Room #2. 'Present in the room are Investigator Ng. N.G. and Ms Cordelia Heath. H.E.A.T.H. I am recording this on a MiniCam 3000 with time and date clearly stamped. Copies of this tape will be supplied on valid request.'

Cordelia's tale was long and sad, yet simple and inspiring. It's true Robbie was violent to her and that he betrayed his gift, but he was a great artist once. He was in trouble over ancient gambling debts. Now that so much money was heading her way, she'd fixed it up. What was 19 thousand dollars? Or 90 thousand? Money was trash. In theory, she had no love left for any part of Robbie. In practice, that was not quite true. She still loved the best parts, the multitudes he carried inside his mind – the transvestite con, the old stonemason, the happy hangman, all of the stage creatures he had created. It was a shame – a tragedy – that one of the multitudes he carried was a wife-basher who couldn't be contained to the stage.

Then again, Cordelia's father had bashed her mother. She knew that demon. It broke her heart to toss Robbie out of her house and out of her life. Oh! the first few months after the separation had been hard. To walk past the vomitous, grey-faced, corpsey drunk – just another street phantom to be stepped over and round – took more courage than she knew she had. 'And yet, Investigator Ng, I will love him until I die. He is the other half of my sad and solitary soul.'

Ng wondered why actors talked so much.

*

Room #3. 'Present in the room are Investigator Ng. N.G. and Mr Yasser Fasser F.A.S.S.E.R. I am recording this on a MiniCam 3000 with time and date clearly stamped. Copies of this tape will be supplied on valid request.'

Yasser played a silent version of the child's game 'Here's the church/here's the steeple/open the door/and here's the people' with his neat tiny fingers. Kidnap? No kidnap. Ask Robbie. Just looking after an old buddy down on his luck. Ask Robbie. No crime to have steel doors. Ask anyone. I didn't pressure the acting lady for money. She offered. Nineteen 'rand to look after him a while. Ask the lady.

Ng made Yasser repeat his story and elaborate on it and Yasser was happy to oblige.

One hour. Then two. At the 140-minute mark, Ng let Yasser and Cordelia go.

*

He even, with Cordelia's blessing, gave the 19 grand back to Yasser.

'Sincere apologies, Miss Heath. All the best. Goodnight to you.'

'Yeah. Sure.' She exits. Dumb pigs.

'I got my eye on you, Fasser,' says Ng quietly. 'If I hear one peep about your being bad, I'll tear that little prison of yours down round your ears with you in it.'

Stella, hidden, listening, feels a tiny thrill run up her back. Even without a gun, little Ng's tough. She decides she likes that.

Fasser swaggers out.

*

Room #1. 'I killed them both,' said Robbie to Ng and Stella as they came in to check on his welfare.

'Who, Mr George? Who did you kill?'

'That black guy, Emu. And the other one, the white guy from TV.'

'I'm stopping this interview at 5.10 am Wednesday. Do you have any objection to being recorded, Mr George?'

'No.'

'Present in the room are Investigator Ng N.G., Miss Stella Pentangeli. P.E.N.T.A.G.E.L.I. and Robert Murray George G.E.O.R.G.E I am recording this on a MiniCam 3000 with time and date clearly stamped. Copies of this tape will be supplied on valid request. Mr George, would you repeat what you just told Miss Pentangeli and me?'

'Sure. I killed them both. Emu and that Google guy from TV.'

Then Robbie started talking and didn't stop. He'd gone

down to The Fortnight and hid in the forest. On the first night he'd crept into Faust Hall. He'd brought a big kitchen knife from the Dog and Pony Hotel where he lived. He found an unlocked door and crept in and killed the first person he saw, Lou Google. He enjoyed it so much the first time he thought he'd hang around for another one. So he went back to the forest and waited until the second night. He couldn't find any open unlocked doors – which made sense – so he tried the shower stalls and got lucky. The door was unlocked and he bashed Emu's head on the tiles again and again and again, then snuck back to the forest and went to stay at Yasser's place.

'The dungeon, you mean?'

'Yeah. Could I please sign a statement now and go to the cells. And could I maybe get some meds and TranQuax or something because I think I'll be in DTs in a couple of hours.'

At which point an SPC quickly worked up a written state-ment and Robbie signed it.

'Have I or anyone involved with the police offered you any inducement or threatened you in any way in order to obtain this confession?' said Ng.

'No. And that's all I'm saying.'

Stella smelt a rat. Robbie stood mute and even Ng couldn't get another word out of him. Did he have help? Was there a second man?

After an hour and more of serene silence, Robbie George, prison playwright and theatre legend in three continents, was assigned a pro bono public defender, charged with two first degree double homicides and led away. Ng got on the phone to the Commander Specialists (Custodial) and told him to make sure Mr George got medical supervision. 'It's important, Commander. He's an acute alcoholic.'

'I'll see to his medication personally, Investigator Ng.'

Specialists (Custodial) don't have much time for bad guy

drunks and their tedious DTs. Left to their own they would have let Robbie cold turkey as best he could and if he got too noisy and the rats and bats flew too low – well, tough shit. He's just a no-good murdering prick.

So, in his neat white holding cell with no sharp edges, a surveillance camera, a concrete bench bed and a dirty moulded plastic toilet, nothing else, Robbie felt the DTs approaching. Unlike Nelson J. Sharp, Robbie wasn't destined for any glorious epiphanies, just pain and terror. Spiders and pink elephants are the stuff of popular legend but for each man and woman it is always a different and fouler delirium.

His legs shot out stiff in front of him just as whatever was in his stomach turned to gruel and he clenched his sphincter too late to stop the filth from flooding out. He was cold yet sweat poured from every part of his body. This was going to be bad.

But Ng knew Custodials and knew the Commander to be useless at just about everything. So he went down to the holding cells of One Police Towers to see Robbie personally. What he saw turned the Investigator into pure loud fury. No one in the Towers had ever seen the legendary Investigator blow like this.

'Fix this man up! Now!'

While the custodials fed Robbie TranQuax and summonsed the locum, Ng stormed into the Commander Specialists (Custodials) office and swore that if he, Ng, ever found his suspects treated like this again, he'd break a few of the Commander's ribs so he'd know about pain. Technically, the Commander out-ranked Ng but the rumour was that Ng was the new Commander Specialists (MVC&IP) and, besides, this version of Ng frankly scared the shit out of the Commander Specialists (Custodials).

This time Robbie George managed to avoid the usual long visit to hell.

Then Ng took Stella to the top of the Towers, to the roof.

19.

up on the roof

One Police Towers has an impressive roof area with a state-of-the-art gas barbecue, picnic tables, a mushroom-shaped pagoda and outdoor furniture. The roof was the only place in the building where the surveillance and recording equipment of Internal Probes were ineffectual. It was off limits in theory to all but the top shelf, but in practice investigators were grudgingly allowed up there with appropriate permissions.

The winter sun hadn't had time to warm the roof yet and there was frost dew everywhere. No wind. View forever. Specialist Probationary Constable Pauline Playne was already waiting.

Pauline's presence was inappropriate, while Citizen Pentangeli's presence was treasonous trespass, if there was such a crime – and if there wasn't there should have been.

Ng knew he could get away with bringing them both here. In the current state of One Police Towers anarchy, he could get away with murder, so to speak.

Neither Ng nor Stella had slept for 24 hours. She could hardly keep her eyes open. Even hardy Ng's face had changed from Asian hue to dead-beat pale. Stella found herself humming a song softly, one from the Angela Drumm portfolio:

Hush little baby
Come sit on my knee.
I'll rock you in my arms.
I'll sing you a song.

I'll give you warm milk.
I'll wrap you up tight.
I'll chase away the boogie man.

Hush little baby
Come sit on my knee
Hush little baby.
Hush.

Huh? Where did that come from? Stella turned off the uninvited Angela in her head and concentrated on Pauline, who looked like she'd slept just fine. Pauline looked back at her. Evil look. Get away from my partner, bitch.

'Constable, I know about you and Miss Heath,' said Ng.

Pauline didn't bat an eyelid. 'I don't know what you're talking about, sir.'

Ng took his MiniCam 3000 from his pocket. 'We have footage of you both at Lady Love. Kissing,' he lied.

'We?'

'Miss Pentangeli and I.'

'Lady Love? What's that?'

'A lesbian bar.'

'Never heard of it, sir.'

'Of course you have.' He waved the MiniCam.

Pauline looked at Stella. Much More Evil look. Then she looked at Ng, but knew she could spend the rest of her life looking at his face and still not be sure whether he was bluffing.

'Ah, what's it matter now?' She wasn't sure if she'd said

that aloud or not. Ever since her affair with Cordelia started, she'd been desperate to brag about it to someone who mattered. In Pauline's small life that was a small list. 'Okay. I love Cordelia. She loves me. So what?'

Ng and Stella both think the same thing at the same time: She sounds like Cordelia already, same black and white and cut and dried. Same 'back off!' Same 'you don't scare me one bit'.

'So. Good,' said Ng patiently. 'As I told Miss Sky, love is good. But Miss Heath is implicated in these events.'

'You've already got your doer! Robbie George, remember?'

Ng ignored this. 'I need to know what information you've passed on to Miss Heath. Pillow talk.'

Pauline glared at Stella, whose mouth went dry.

Ng thinks Robbie is innocent!

'I see,' Pauline said bitterly.

'You see what?'

'I see you think the only reason Cordelia would want me is to get information about her bloody ex-husband to keep the wife-beating son of a bitch out of prison. You're wrong. I haven't told her anything and she never asked. We speak only the language of love.'

Ouch. Ng affected surprise. 'Didn't Miss Heath want to know, say, how the investigations were getting on?'

'No.'

'Didn't want to know if she was a suspect?'

'No.'

'Funny.'

'What's funny?'

'She loves you, yes?'

'So?'

'And you love her?'

'Yes. So?'

'Pauline, people she knows have been killed. Her ex-husband's been charged. Doesn't she ask – even once – how your day has gone? How things go at the office? What's the gossip on the Bushy Creek murders? It's normal. It's part of love.'

'No.'

'You called Mr George "a wife-beating son of a bitch". Why? Who told you he was a wife-beating son of a bitch?' No reply. 'They're not words you use. They're Miss Heath's words, surely.'

'So?'

'So you've become very close very quickly. It would be normal to share your lives.' He fixed his gaze on her. 'When did Miss Heath seduce you? The first time?'

'I forget.'

Stella waited, not daring to breathe. Something – someone – was about to break.

'I suggest it was Tuesday night. Midnight, perhaps one o'clock. The time of the second murder.' Pauline said nothing. 'When she came to your room, did Miss Heath seem agitated?'

'Of course she was agitated. She'd come to seduce me. *I* was agitated.'

'Was she wet?'

'Wet?'

'Were her clothes wet?'

'You mean had she been wrestling with Emu Gentle in the shower block bashing his head on the floor? No. Her clothes were dry.'

'Was her hair dry?'

Bingo! That was the thought Pauline had been trying to bury way down in the well of her mind. 'She'd just washed it.'

'In the shower block?'

'In her room sink.'

Ng bored in. 'Later, back here in the city she told you something, didn't she?'

Pause. 'Yes.'

'She told you Mr George had killed both clients, didn't she?' Pauline stays silent but she nods. 'Did she actually see him kill Mr Google or Mr Emu?'

'No. All she knew was he was round about, hiding in the forest, and that he was capable of murder. "Eager" to murder was her word.'

There was no wind on the roof. This high up, there should be a breeze. But it was still for a long time.

'I would have come forward – about the Robbie George evidence – but it wasn't necessary. And I love her.' She said it simply and matter-of-factly.

Ng went on. 'Did Miss Heath tell you why Mr George did it?'

'She thinks he came to rob the rooms and maybe panicked. He owes money. Gambling debts. To Doc Mortaferi.'

Ng continued gently: 'Pauline – if I asked you not see Miss Heath, what would you say?'

'No.'

'Just until this is behind us.'

'No. That's what I'd say. No. I'd say I quit. Arrest me. Fuck you. Fuck you all.' Cordelia was back inside the Constable.

Ng nodded as if he'd expected no different. The air grew even stiller, trying to eavesdrop. Finally:

'You won't tell Miss Heath about this talk?'

'No sir. I promise.'

'Then let's forget it. I brought you up here so we'd have privacy. So this could be between you and me.'

'What about her?' Evil look at Stella.

'Miss Pentangeli is a consultant on these events. What's been said here stays here.'

'Pauline, I swear nothing leaves this roof.'

'Thank you.'

129

Pauline headed for the lift, powered by some of the grace she'd borrowed from her beautiful and formidable lover, her back straight and strong. The lift door opened and she was whisked away.

'What do you think, Stella?'

'Truth?'

'Please.'

'She'll tell Cordelia.'

'I hope so. I'm counting on it.'

20.

dreams

ROBBIE DID IT!! OFFICIAL!

*ROBBIE GEORGE SILENT ABOUT MYSTERIOUS
'SECOND MAN'!*

*NG: 'WE MAY NEVER KNOW WHO THE SECOND
MAN WAS.'*

*SHOWBIZ! SHOWBIZ! SHOWBIZ! ONLINE!
THE PENTANGELI PAPERS *EXCLUSIVE*
ROBBIE CONFESSES!*
*Police are now certain that Robbie George, the prison playwright,
is guilty of the so-called Murders at The Fortnight.*

Near noon, Stella's V-dub pulled up outside the Best Rest
Motel in dingy old East Sweethurst. 'What are we doing here?'
'I live here,' said Ng and waited. Stella didn't disappoint.
She looked at the grey and sour cream motel with its dirty
wide parking spaces and buzzy flickery red sign. Best Rest –
Best Rest – Weekly Rates – Weekly Rates. Someone had for-
gotten to turn it off. The place had an air of resigned misery
and too many sordid tales told too many times.

'You *live* here?' It was a dump. A few battered cars were parked outside a few battered doors.

'It's not as bad as it looks.'

'It couldn't be.'

'It's close to trains and buses. I get a reduced rate. They like having a police person in residence.'

'Jesus, Ng.'

Ng. Normally, the Investigator would have pounced on the use of his name without adornment but he liked it.

Ng.

He hadn't noticed when she'd started to use just his surname. It sounded . . . intimate.

He opened the V-dub's door. 'Thank you for everything, Stella. You've been a great help.' He got out. Pause. 'Well, bye.'

Pause. 'Bye.'

'Maybe I'll see you around. A drink. Coffee.' This was Ng's idea of wooing.

'Hope so.' That was a coy Stella come-on.

'You know where I am.'

'You too.'

'Bye.'

'Bye.'

'Bye.'

With a wave, Stella gunned the V-dub and was gone.

*

Ng's Room 11 was on the ground floor with an uninterrupted view of pocked asphalt, cheap cars and a thin sick tree embedded in concrete outside his door. His garden.

Ng wasn't lying when he said he liked it at Best Rest. Except in the area of crime, his daily passage through life left few marks. Mrs Puccini, the owner, or her idiot son Ned came twice weekly to 'freshen things up'. But they had little to do, the room being spotless always. Fresh sheets and towels twice a week and full use of the main kitchen. He'd gotten Specialists (Security) to burglar-proof the room and installed a small but heavy safe for his documents and laptop. It would take three junkies with strong backs to haul it away and junkies don't have strong backs. He'd brought only two pieces of furniture – a long squat bookcase which was full to overflowing and a stuffed comfy black leather armchair – otherwise happy to use the motel's hardy and utilitarian as-founds.

Ng had reached a stage in his life where he could either start accumulating a thousand comforts for his middle and late age or he could start shedding them.

He went to the tiny bathroom where the tray was piled with tea bags and tiny coffee satchels, turned on the electric jug, then turned it off again, realised he was about to pass out from fatigue, checked the lock, took off his clothes and . . .

Crash!

He didn't dream. He seldom did. It hurt.

*

Stella was too tired to undress. She flung her shoes off, climbed into her bed and she . . .

Crash!

She dreamed a detective dream. Usually her dreams were mad with wild chases, ogres, erotica, beautiful creatures. This time she saw two ghosts – Lou Google and Emu Gentle – standing at a black door, looking at her accusingly. Lou's chest was bloody. Emu's head was bashed in at the back. They said in unison: 'Robbie didn't do it.'

Then Nelson Sharp, Robbie George, Cordelia Heath, Jeddah Magnum, Lucy Sky, Yasser Fasser and Pauline Playne came in through the door, each with a number on their chest. They said, 'Robbie didn't do it.'

Behind them were the Fortnighters – a million or more. They too said, 'Robbie didn't do it.'

Angela Drumm came in with her guitar and sang a new song with only one line:

Robbie didn't do it.

which she sang over and over again. Then lights came on which were like spotlights except they flashed Best Rest – Weekly Rates – Robbie Didn't Do It – Best Rest – Weekly Rates – Robbie Didn't Do It – Best Rest – Weekly Rates – Robbie Didn't Do It.

21.

weird! wacky#! and
wonderful##!

A picture's worth a thousand words, all right. Stella, Deb, Debbi or Derek could have written for a decade about the final hours of The Fortnight, but it wouldn't have captured as perfectly the madness, grief and terror as did the two minutes and 16 seconds of footage being snickered over and downloaded by a million internet users. Two minutes and sixteen seconds of Jeddah Magnum wandering madly naked through the corridors of Faust Hall, laughing. Jeddah The Hutt. Hard as Deb had tried, someone – the camera guy? the sound woman? – had preserved the moment and decided to share the joke with the world by uploading it to the Weird! Wacky#! And Wonderful##! site. Now 'The Mad Jeddah' tape was everywhere.

Word soon got round the Bushy Creek Caravan and Mobile Home Park about the tape. Before this, Jeddah had been regarded as a well-meaning eccentric who'd contributed much to the local community, not least as the founder, chair and artistic director of the Bushy Creek Young Theatre Players, a surprisingly good youth group. She was voted off the Theatre Players board unanimously when the tape surfaced.

An enterprising kid from Lot 66 managed to make some

pocket money by drilling a hole in the convenience block right where Jeddah was accustomed to taking her morning shower. The 'Mad Jeddah Freak Show' scam didn't last long since the park maintenance man was ever vigilant when it came to the convenience blocks.

*

Ten days after the first murder at The Fortnight, Stella was back in Bushy Creek. She'd found out about the tape via her Sweethurst Caff sit-down with Terry. One of the Caff characters chose that moment to play his Mad Jeddah DVD on the Caff TV. Stella pulled out the plug and swore she'd shove it up the arse of the first person who tried that again. For once, the Caff was silent.

She tried getting Jeddah on her mobile but it was turned off. She tried ringing the caravan park office but was icily informed by the secretary (a rabid anti-Jeddahite) that private calls and messages were *never* passed on unless it was an emergency, which this wasn't. Finally, Stella drove the three hours to Bushy Creek and parked outside Jeddah's faux Romany van.

'Jeddah!'

No answer. Stella tried knocking and hollering, then decided she'd scour the town.

'I can't come out, Stells. I just can't.'

Stella hurried back to the door. 'Let me in Jeds. Please.'

'No.'

Silence.

'You're not going to do anything silly, are you, Jeds?'

'No.'

'Promise?'

'Yes.'

'Let me in. I won't even speak.'

'No.'

Silence.

'Tell you what, Jeddah. I'll stay overnight at the motel, all right? You ring me there. Okay?' Silence. 'Did you hear me? The motel?'

'You don't have to do that.'

'Ring me. Anytime.' Silence. 'Jeddah?' Silence.

Finally, with a few glares piercing her back, Stella gunned out of the park and booked into the hotel with a pizza and a bottle of Beefeater but Jeddah didn't ring.

Next morning, on her way back to the city, Stella stopped in at Jeddah's van. Before she could raise her hand to knock, Jeddah erupted out the tiny door and enveloped Stella in a huge, painful hug.

'Only *you* came, Stella. Only you.'

Stella never got a clear look at Jeddah's face before she was back inside the closed van again.

*

Jeddah would just look at herself over and over again.

Jeddah The Hutt.

Mad Jeddah.

Lady MadBeth.

She'd rewind the tape on the tiny monitor and play it again, her face set in stone.

22.

milton

SHOWBIZ! SHOWBIZ! SHOWBIZ! ONLINE!
THE PENTANGELI PAPERS *EXCLUSIVE*
SURPRISE FORTNIGHT BLOCKBUSTER!!
HOLLYWOOD HOT SHOTS ON THE TRAIL!!
CORDELIA HEATH'S FIRST PLAY A TRIUMPH!
It sounds like the plot for 'A Star Is Born' but Milton . . .

Milton Shaver liked to think of himself as evil. Not just bad or sinful. Evil. If there was an evil warlock prince, a netherworld beast who walked the showbiz parts of earth in human form, a fiend who fell from grace with God, Milton Shaver, ace Hollywood player, liked to think it was he.

Had Milton Shaver fallen to earth with Lucifer, he liked to think he would have immediately shown the Evil One who was boss. What's more Lucifer would have taken the hint. Satan would have said, 'I shall roam the earth entire as like a roaring lion! But you can have showbiz.'

Milton was a much richer, much more powerful Lou Google – turbo-charged and even nastier. Tyrant that Lou had been, he was to Milton Shaver as a kindergarten bully is to Joseph Stalin. The economics of showbiz had, until recently, kept Milton at bay. Fly out from LA for short, bloody feedings on helpless movie and TV throats. Suck 'em dry, fly back to Bev Hills.

Butte, Oxford, Sydney, Lima, Cape Town, Papeete – didn't matter. Suck 'em dry.

Lou Google died in his prime, while his name still meant fear and his tribe still ruled its tiny territory. Perhaps, in a weird way, Lou was lucky to have been slain when he was – for Lou's day was fast coming to an end. The Miltons had smelt new blood.

*

Milton Shaver hadn't really fallen from heaven with Lucifer.

'I was born in Holcomb, Kansas, a small town where the horrendous murder of an entire innocent family – chronicled in Truman Capote's magnificent book and movie *In Cold Blood* – had famously occurred. But, I didn't do it, he he.'

Milton would drop these tidbits into interviews with media for several reasons. 1. To show he was from poor but honest stock. 2. To show he knew about the darker side of bucolic life. 3. To show he knew who Truman Capote was – i.e. that he read books. 4. To throw the dumb fucks off the scent.

In fact, every word was a lie. Holcomb Shmolcomb. He'd been born and bred in New Jersey by poor but dishonest small-time heroin distributors and the only reason they were poor was they kept dipping into the product. The father died first (OD), then the mother (AIDS). Milton was a natural for showbiz.

As soon as Emu Gentle was murdered, Milton's minions had brought word of the hideous slaughter, along with – much better – rumours of a brilliant new play script 'Midwinter dreams of a dead black man', the workshopping of which had been the superstar-turned-activist's final strut on the fretful stage of life.

Milton smelt a good movie. He faxed, then emailed, then rang Cordelia Heath all the way from Bev Hills and offered to take over all negotiations.

'Look, Ms Heath,' he had plunged right in, 'we got us a black murdered naked superstar. There's a teevemovie *and* a feature film in all this. Star turns back on fame, goes back to help his people nada nada nada and gets killed! This is the "Oh life! what a sting you have!" stuff the punters love. Then there's this play of yours. We got stage, we got TV, we got film.'

Writers and actors can spend a fruitless lifetime trying to get a Hollywood agent. Milton Shaver was offering his services to Cordelia Heath right now. What did Cordelia think? Did she want to dance with the man from Holcomb?

'Yes.'

'I take 25 per cent of gross. Non-negotiable. Take it or leave it.'

'I take it.'

'Good choice. I guarantee I can turn you from a Mudville writelette into a Hollywood player. Writer. Actor. Whatever. They'll bury you if you don't get someone like me. Now Cordelia, I don't require a contract. A handshake's fine.'

The subtext was, of course: 'I'm a shark, doll. Better I should not decide you're my breakfast.' The subtext was: 'I'm on your team and, believe me, you *do not* want me on anyone else's team playing agin ya.' The final, bottom-line, truth-of-the-matter subtext was: 'I have a made an obscene amount of money out of brokering mega-deals and shepherding mega-stars. If you bust my balls, I'll rip your ovaries out and feed them to my Rottweiler.'

*

There's an old saying – a conservative is a liberal who's been mugged.

'Cordelia's been mugged by life once too often.'

Once upon a time she had toured factories to inflict workers' theatre on workers so they'd rise up against dogs like Milton. She'd toiled endlessly in prisons – built by dogs like Milton – to rescue Robbie Georges from an artless hell.

Now . . .

Milton Shaver?

'It's Snow White and The Big Bad Wolf.'

'It's Saint Cordelia and The Dragon.'

'That greasy fucking suckerfish is Cordelia's agent?'

23.

week of the pig

A week passes. Life settles down in Stella's Sweethurst universe. *The Pentangeli Papers* forges ahead. The stats, hits, posts, downloads, subs climb steadily. A rumour sweeps the zine scene that *TPP* is about to be listed in the top 10 arts sites.

On the media front, the title 'Bushy Creek Celebrity Slayings' has inched out 'Murders at The Fortnight' (too arcane) as the official *nom de crime* and, since Derek had come up with the moniker, he collects a half dozen 10-dollar side bets from colleagues. Now that both the Google and Gentle funerals have come and gone, the story seems to be as dead as they are.

The dirty bastards at *Hard Currently* try to milk it by bribing some screws to bug Robbie George. But Robbie never talks about the murders. In fact he doesn't talk at all. He seems to be living in a place inside his head where visitors are unwelcome. *Hard Currently* tries to get some of its money back:

STONE SILENCE FROM STONE COLD KILLER!

and:

SERIAL KILLER SCRIBE SHROUDED IN
SUICIDAL SILENCE!

Hard Currently, *North East West South* and *Night Night* must have taken their eyes off the ball since neither Derek nor Debbi nor even Deb notice the release from City Mental of the young actor turned prophet Nelson J. Sharp. Resumption of Nelson's meds has brought him out of his manic religious phase. He now agrees with his doctors that 'the notion of the Judaeo-Christian deity YHWH physically intervening in my life is ridiculous'.

'The Age of Miracles ceased round the second or third century AD,' the shrink had said.

'That's right, doc.'

'The Fortnight is not some bizarre code for an all-new improved Armageddon, right?'

'Of course not. Ho ho ho.'

'And a man having nine fingers doesn't necessarily mean we have to get out our Book of Revelation, right?'

'Please, doc, you're embarrassing me. Ha ha ha.'

'Off you go, Nelson.'

Cured in a week. Is there anything psychotropic drugs can't do?

*

Ng visits Robbie George in prison several times but can't make him talk. Robbie feels his confession sufficient explanation, and everyone agrees except the Investigator.

'Why go all the way to Bushy Creek, Mr George?' Silence. 'Why hide in the forest? Why kill? Why kill these people, in particular?' Silence. 'You must have planned murder, else why steal a knife from the hotel kitchen?' Silence. 'Why kill Emu Gentle? You admired him. I've read in articles, interviews, many of them how you admired him. Why?' Silence.

Each visit, as Ng starts to leave Robbie rouses himself from his – depression? catatonia? masochistic reverie? – to thank Ng for coming down hard on the guards and making his

143

DTs bearable. Then he clams up as if to say more would become addictive.

*

In the showbiz arena, Cordelia isn't the only Big Winner. Radio, newspapers, zines suddenly find Lucy Sky hip. She finds herself besieged by TV producers. She's first cab off the rank if *North East West South* or *Hard Currently* or *Night Night* want a talking head (with a firm and pouting bosom) to do a background/follow-up/update/colour piece on the Bushy Creek Celebrity Murders.

Her first paid gig – barely 48 hours after coming home – is at the Sweethurst Caff Back Garden Wednesday Evening Blues and Folk Nite where, to the chagrin of her siblings and the delight of Mum and Dad, she slays 'em! Murders 'em! She sings 'Killer Love', 'Lonely Little Room' and 'Hush Little Baby'. When she runs out of Angela Drumm songs she sings 'Black Man', in honour of her good friend, the late great Emu Gentle. She sings show tunes and blues. She writes a new song just like that.

> *Come senators, businessmen, listen up big.*
> *There's things goin' down that you'll never dig.*
> *The Year of the Rat,*
> *The Week of the Pig.*
>
> *Oink and squeak,*
> *oink and squeak*
> *No need to speak,*
> *no need to speak.*
>
> *Can't you hear it?*
> *Don't you dig?*

Year of the Rat,
Week of the Pig.

Maybe she's a genius, think the elite of Sweethurst who adopt the young songstress with the passion they had a decade or two back for baby seals.

Anyone in showbiz might have told her (and does) that PR and adulation are the best cures for sadness. Temporary but total. Later on, PR and adulation transmute into a bitterer sadness but don't worry about that yet, honey. Lie back and think of You. And they might have told her (and do) that it is helpful she is a good singer but not strictly necessary. Looks and youth combined with her association with Saint Emu have polished her image into the shiny shape of a no-longer-just-wannabe. Her player potential is now a comer with a bullet.

*

Jeddah Magnum still doesn't venture far from her caravan. A few of the more thoughtful armchair showbiz sleuths have her pegged as the real killer.

'She's got the motive and the muscle. Lou was TV! TV's always been Jeddah's enemy! As for Emu, that was lust gone wrong.'

'Sure. She sat on poor Emu's face and crushed the poor bastard's skull, ho ho.'

Actually, *tout le showbiz* would be surprised how seriously Investigator Ng is treating Jeddah's possible guilt. His inquiries about Jeddah and several of these very jokesters themselves are conducted softy softly but with efficiency. Which – had they known and had the wit to wonder – would suggest a paradox. If the confessed murderer is already locked up, why is Ng still sniffing around?

*

145

Conscience make cowards of us, but so does fear of rejection. Ng looms in the forefront of Stella's mind. His attractive melancholy, his dry-to-the-point-of-astringent sense of humour, his basic decency, his slim body, the sexiness of power and competence.

Yummy.

She's gone as far as she dares in making it obvious she's available. She even asks a cop who knows him to tell Ng how comfy her home is, how roomy, how her *home-cooked meals* used to be the talk of showbiz gourmets and anytime Ng felt hungry . . .

One night with Lou Google had turned her taps back on and she's ripe for a good plumber. So why doesn't the son of a bitch ring her?

*

Ng finds his mind drifting often towards Stella. Since the break-up of his marriage, he has increasingly involved himself in home-movie-making with his precious MiniCam 3000. Short experimental pieces. Just for fun. The sort of fun, however, that a bachelor of a certain age can easily find turning into an obsession – into yet another excuse for non-engagement with the real world.

Stella has awoken the slumbering beast, so to speak, and it has confused and troubled him. The beast is more trouble than it's worth sometimes.

And yet, in his more feminine moments he pictures himself as a male Pauline Playne, lying on his bed, hearing a 'knock knock it's me' on the door and opening it to find Stella with champagne bottle in hand intent on seducing him Cordelia-style right there and then whether he likes it or not. In matters of the heart, Ng is a man who mistakes impenetrability for subtlety. When – in plain view and close earshot of Civilian Pentangeli – he absolved Specialist Probationary Constable

Playne and Minor Suspect Heath from official censure for their sexual liaison, he had been sending a signal to Stella that it would be okay for her to similarly liaise with, say, him.

So why didn't the silly woman ring him?

*

Specialist Probationary Constable Playne is a bundle of secrets. She can't tell Cordelia about the roof-top chat with Ng, but she does anyway. Breaking her word to the Investigator is another secret. She can't talk to her colleagues and her pitifully few friends about her poopsie until the Gentle/Google trial is finished. She makes the mistake of telling her mother – a sweet grey-haired apple-cheeked lady – and her father – a grey-haired gent of amiable disposition – about Cordelia.

'It's love, Mummy. It's real love, Daddy!'

Mother and father freak. They weep tears of shame at the horror of it all. Mother howls to the Virgin Mary, Comforter of the Afflicted: 'Please intercede with Your Son so He will take this demon of unnatural lust out of our baby girl.'

Father mourns: 'Oh Holy Ghost make sure our wicked daughter won't burn for all eternity in the fires of Hell!'

They urge Pauline to see a priest and confess, then see a shrink and confess. They beg beg beg her 'not to see that Jezebel and to stop doing *that* to *anyone female*!'

Secrets. To top all that off, Pauline carries round a brilliant non-crime-related secret which poopsie makes her promise not to tell – Milton Shaver has arrived in town! He's staying at La Grande Étoile in the Louis XIV Suite neck-deep in Cordelia Heath's blossoming career – doing deals and taking meetings and accepting bids and upping waiver fees.

Hollywood keeps calling. With little effort, Milton has convinced LA-LA that, given the notoriety of poor Emu's demise, 'Midnight dreams of a dead black man' might be a goer.

Cordelia and Pauline reel in shock at the sheer size of the numbers being bandied around. Cordelia's big payday starts at close to a million dollars and is rapidly heading north.

*

The fact that Milton is a crook in all but name means nothing to Pauline. He's a Hollywood thug, brute, bullyboy and stand-over man. So? The Law says he's a cleanskin. In her time – like every police person who's ever lived – she's seen her colleagues act thuggy and brutal and bullyboy. The Law says they're not crims, they're cops. And if this Shaver clown can help make Cordelia happy, then . . . go for it!

All Pauline wants is for Cordelia to stop crying out in the night and stop waking up bathed in sweat so that Pauline must rub her down with soft-as-clouds towels and croon her back to sleep.

In short, all Specialist Probationary Constable Pauline Playne wants is for her lover not to be sad.

24.

dog and pony

During his inquiries, one of Ng's seemingly worldwide consortium of snitches fed the Investigator an interesting fact. A few years back in LA, Milton Shaver had wanted Emu Gentle to join his agency but Emu had laughed in his face — a very dangerous move. Shaver had been furious. Ng's contacts in the LAPD, LASO and FBI tracked down Shaver's movements, mobile calls and emails the previous week.

He was innocent. Of these murders at least.

*

Stella, as usual, placed a lot of faith in her dry mouth and it was working overtime.

#1. Robbie George. He'd said he'd brought a big kitchen knife with him from the hotel he lived in. Which meant Jeddah was lying when she said the knife was hers.

#2. Robbie said he'd crept into Faust Hall, found Stella's door unlocked, crept in and killed the first person he saw. Luckily it was Lou Google, not her. For Emu's murder, he went back to the forest and waited until the next night, when he got lucky with the shower stalls. He bashed Emu's head on the tiles and snuck silently back to the forest.

Yeah, well, maybe. Perhaps all that master crim stuff was possible for a master crim or even an enthusiastic amateur. But *Robbie George?* The guy had forgotten what it was like to walk in a straight line. He would have been bouncing off the Faust Hall residential walls like a basketball, not making his way cat-like through halls of murder.

#3. Yasser Fasser. He knew where and when to pick Robbie up. How? Who told him? Stella knew a city folk when she saw one and she saw one in Yasser Fasser. If he was in the vicinity of Bushy Creek it wasn't to admire nature. Someone had sent him to fetch Robbie. Who? Why?

#4. TranQuax and Stella. Ng had told her she'd had at least six standard doses of TranQuax in her blood. *It's too much. Lou would drop one, maybe two in my drinks. He wanted to seduce me, not make me comatose.* Why so many drugs?

#5. TranQuax and Lou. 'Mr Google ... had a larger dosage of TranQuax. Much larger.' Why? If Lou wanted to ravish her (and he certainly did) why nearly drug himself to noddy land?

#6. TranQuax and the stash. Someone had left a huge stash of TranQuax in her luggage and even spiked a Beefeater bottle with the stuff. Why? To frame her. All that takes planning – i.e. brain cells. Did Robbie have enough cells left?

*

Robbie's home, The Dog and Pony Hotel, had been elegant 80 years ago, then quaint, and now was a two-storey inner city rathole, a residential cemetery for corpses who weren't quite dead yet. There were a score or so poker machines that flashed and went PING! and YAWWWW! WANG POIM!! all day every day but the drunkies hardly noticed. Deb, Debbie, Derek and other media snoops had already combed Robbie's room for clues, but Stella guessed they'd have been too late. She figured that once Robbie had been named and incarcerated, the drunks would have stripped his room.

The publican and his missus were bluff and friendly types. 'Sure. Snoop around, lady. Do what you gotta do. Just spell the name right.'

'Were there any large kitchen knives stolen round about the time Robbie left?' Given that no one in their right mind would voluntarily eat at the Dog and Pony, the pub had a very limited supply of kitchenalia.

'Sorry, lady, no knives are missing. Definitely. Positively.' They were cheerily adamant about it. So the knife was Jeddah's. Why did Robbie lie about it being his?

As Stella was leaving, a drunk sidled up to her and whispered in her face. *Eee-uw! The breath!* 'I'm real glad the cops sent a whitey to look round this time. They sent some short arse Chink a couple of hours ago. Don't like them Chinks. Even the little ones.'

So Ng had been here too.

*

Stella sat in her car outside the Dog and Pony and weighed her options. She didn't fancy making a return visit to Yasser Fasser. Not without a tank. But it had to be done. *Someone* had told Fasser where Robbie George would be on the morning after Emu's murder. That someone had told Fasser to snatch Robbie and keep him locked up for a while. That someone was the shadowy second party Stella's dry mouth told her was floating round the edges of these murders.

She wasn't going to find out sitting here. After all, she'd bravely entered the Bushy Creek forest all alone. She'd lived through a murder in her very own bed and another murder in the very next shower cubicle. She was a showbiz detective hero, for Chrissakes! Avanti!

A hand reached into her V-dub window and touched her shoulder.

'Ahhh!'

'Forgive me for startling you.'

It was Ng. 'What is it with you? You *like* hearing me scream?'

Ng pondered the question.

'No.'

'What are you doing here?'

'I gather you've discovered that Mr George didn't steal a knife.' She nodded brusquely. 'Why, I wonder, did Mr George lie about that?'

'My thoughts exactly. Maybe he's taking the blame for the event. For both events.' Events? Jesus, Stella thought, I'm starting to talk like a police person.

'Stella, does it seem to you more and more that Mr George is a rather a Lee Harvey Oswald figure? The right man in the wrong place at the right time?'

'Yes it does.'

'If you don't mind my asking – where are you going?'

'To see that Fasser creep.'

'Why?'

'To find out who sent Fasser to imprison Robbie.'

'But we know that already.'

'We do?'

'Mr George's one connection to the criminal classes is his predilection for gambling. Mr Fasser's connection to Mr George is Doc Mortaferi. Mr Fasser would never do a kidnap without permission from Mortaferi. Why don't you go straight to the top?'

'You mean visit Mortaferi?'

'Why not?'

'Cos he's Mr Big and he scares me.'

'I have to make a phone call. Then I'll come with you.'

'I'll be okay.'

'Please,' he said. 'With someone like Mortaferi, even I get a bit scared.'

I wonder if you really do, you tough little bastard.

25.

moriarty

Angela Drumm's classic song played in Stella's head all the
way to Doc Mortaferi's.

> *I been tracking you down*
> *like Sherlock Holmes, sleuth.*
> *I was hired by Cupid*
> *sometime in my youth.*
>
> *'Find a Moriarty,'*
> *Cupid said.*
> *'Bring him on back.*
> *Alive or dead.*
>
> *'He may be a bad man.*
> *That's elementary.*
> *But you can find him easy as*
> *One, two, three.*
>
> *'One, two, three.*
> *One, two, three.*

Sherlock Holmes, man,
Got nothin on you.'

I grabbed his balls
At Reichenbach Falls.
1, 3, 2.
1, 2, 3.
Sherlock Holmes, man,
Got nothin' on me.

*

Doc's New Gothic eleven-bedroom beach 'villa mansion' stood high on a promontory overlooking Bayside Bay – just high enough up to scar the natural beauty of the bay and just big enough to require total demolition to make amends. As Ng and Stella headed for the massive oak doors, Ng said softly, 'Don't be fooled. Mortaferi wants to be seen as some kind of Robin Hood. He has politicians and police in his pocket. He tosses a bit of blood money at a few charities and the media think that makes him Santa Claus. He's not. He's . . .'

'He's your White Whale, isn't he, Cap'n Ahab?' Stella interrupted, suddenly clear. 'He's your Moriarty, isn't he, Holmes? "Doc Mortaferi", "Professor Moriarty". They even sound the same.' Ng stopped her just feet from the main door. Stella had been kidding but Ng, she saw, was not. His face was beyond hard, his eyes beyond hate.

'Mortaferi's not some romantic Napoleon of Crime, Stella. He kills people and he's killing this city. One day he'll pay.'

Stella shivered even though here, at Bayside Bay, the sun always shone and the wind was always balmy.

The door opened. Doc Mortaferi was a large muscly man with a dark, nouveau-riche tan that promised melanoma further down the line. 'Come in, come in, come in. I thought it was you, Investigator,' he said. Drink in hand, he ushered them into the 'bottom deck lounge' – all white and black furnishings and 240-degree sea views. What looked like an English butler entered.

'Drinks?'

Ng: 'No.'

Mortaferi: 'Miss Pentangeli?'

'You know my name?' Stella didn't like the sound of that. 'Could I bother you for gin? Beefeater? Neat? Double?'

The butler was back almost before the words were out, handing Mortaferi the bucket-sized gin so the host could make the gracious gesture of handing it to her personally. Stella didn't bother feigning her usual just-the-one this time. *Mr Big knows my fucking name?*

Mortaferi nodded to the butler, who exited gracefully, almost but not quite bowing.

Ng was suddenly all business. 'I won't waste your time, Mortaferi.'

'Doc, Mr Ng. People call me Doc.'

'I don't call you Doc. Fools call you Doc because your speciality is murder. It's a joke. Like you. Except I never got it.'

Steam rose off Mortaferi and Stella sensed he wouldn't consider killing police off-limits.

After long seconds, Mortaferi swallowed his bile. 'Investigator Ng, I pride myself on my hospitality. No visit from you could be called "wasting my time". You can waste all the time you like. Time is what the good Lord gives us instead of diamonds.'

'I know you often hire Yasser Fasser to maim, imprison and murder your opponents.' Christ! thought Stella, Ng wants this psycho to do us. 'You had Robbie George, the playwright, imprisoned. I want to know why. Now.'

Mortaferi looked at Ng and decided. 'Alfred,' he murmured.

The butler entered with two men, each about seven feet tall and six feet wide. The wide boys carried great big guns aimed at Ng and Stella who, ridiculously, could only wonder if Alfred was the butler's real name.

'Mr Ng,' said Doc, his voice dark and low, 'I hate the fact that you've been sniffing around my business and my house. I hate that a man sees fit to treat me rudely in my *own fucking home*! I hate it that you're too stupid to leave me alone.'

Alfred removed Ng's tiny handgun from the Investigator's small-of-the-back holster and patted him down. When he was finished, Doc went on, 'You're not a herd animal, Mr Ng. That makes you weak. Men like me can pick you off and the herd won't be upset. Know what I mean?'

'I do indeed,' said Ng as though conceding a fine debating point, then moved to Mortaferi and slapped his face with an open hand. The Doc's eyes filled with blood.

Yet again, Stella's bowels turned to water. She vowed she'd give up this lady showbiz detective crap if only the good Lord would get her out of this.

She watched as Ng sat down on a cushy armchair. The butler and the wide boys looked as though they weren't sure what they'd seen, but they'd seen it all right and now Mortaferi had no choice. He opened his mouth to order the hit.

Ng silenced him with an authoritative hand. 'Not in here, Mortaferi – surely.' He spoke to them all yet was looking serenely out to sea. 'I know how it works. You take Miss Pentangeli and me outside to the boat house.' He pointed to a small faux Tahitian shed at the edge of the cliff. 'You do your murders there. Tiles. Easy to remove the stains.'

Stella started saying a Hail Mary. *We're dead. For sure.*

'You take our bodies out in the boat. Weigh us down. Drop us over the side. That's how it goes isn't it? Except for Tiny Malloy – you hacked him up and stuffed him in a bar fridge *then* dropped him overboard. So the sharks wouldn't get him. Out of respect, I understand.'

'You know about Tiny?' Mortaferi looked peeved.

As usual, Ng didn't exactly answer the question. 'One good point about not being a – as you say – "herd animal",' he said, 'is sometimes you know things the herd doesn't. So if a piece of human shit like, say, you, had a police chief on his payroll – someone like, say, Specialists Co-ordinator Chief Wherring, or, say, City Area Commander Sawtell, or if a politician like, say, Jack O'Sullivan owed you gambling money or if you had photos of, say, Deputy Speaker Linstead, with several of your girls, and . . .'

Christ, thought Stella, this sentence will never end. But it did. Right then. Ng moved to the huge seaward window and made a small gesture. He stepped aside and suddenly TINKLE! WING! a bullet from a high-powered rifle shattered the window and buried itself in one of the lush sofas.

'Shit!' said Mortaferi or maybe it was the butler or the wide boys. Ng made a small motion again and again TINKLE! WING! another bullet smashed its way into Doc Mortaferi's fortress as though Ng had a choir of armed angels at his beck and call.

To Mortaferi's credit he did not hit the ground in a cowardly manner like Alfred and the wide boys. White-faced as he was, he stood his ground.

Ng half-turned towards the help. 'You three. Put down all the guns and leave.'

Mortaferi nodded at them but he needn't have bothered. They were already meekly obeying and vanishing. The Doc exploded. 'You dare? You dare to fucking shoot up my *home*?'

Stella opted for a sassy wisecrack. 'Don't ask Ng questions, Mr Mortaferi. He never answers them.' Both men looked at her. Ng, with the eye furtherest from Mortaferi, winked at her.

'So, Mortaferi – you, Yasser Fasser and Robbie George – tell me about it.'

Mortaferi hesitated. He looked at the two spidery fractures in his so-called bullet-proof glass.

Finally he spoke. 'Off the record?'

'Yes.'

'No charges?'

'None.'

'You taping this?'

'No.'

'What about her?'

'She's with me.'

Stella didn't know what she was saying but she said it anyway: 'You have my word.'

For an instant Mortaferi looked ready to lie, then a light went out behind his eyes and he started talking.

'It's silly, really but I'd always felt bad about the pissy little nineteen grand Robbie owed me. It wasn't the money so much – it was the cheek of the man. Even hacking off his finger didn't satisfy. Didn't send a firm enough message, you know? So, every now and again, I'd send a boy to slap Robbie around, loosen some teeth, you know – but Robbie was stone broke, so what can a man do? In the end, I thought I'd just eat the loss and the lack of respect.

'Then, root me rigid, about three months ago, Robbie rolls up here, bold as brass. He sits where you're sitting now, Mr Ng. He says he has a proposition for me. "What is it?" says I. He says he wants me to finance a scheme and provide some logistical assistance. He wants to go rob this Fortnight wank. He'll hole up in some forest nearby and spend a few days robbing the rooms. He figures he can get back the nineteen grand and keep the change.'

'What sort of logistical assistance?'

'Not much. A ride down. A ride back. A few flagons of that shitty booze he liked.'

'Bloodspoor's,' Stella piped up.

'Right. Bloodspoor's.'

Mortaferi grinned sheepishly, his blazing white teeth flashing from mahogany skin. 'You must understand, Mr Ng, this had been *embarrassing* for me. Macca, Lee, Wolfman – all the boys – they'd keep bringing it up. "Some crim you are, Doc, letting a wino get the drop on you." You understand.'

Ng nodded. Of course. Mortifying.

'So I said yeah, okay, Robbie. I got Fasser to drive him down, then drive him back.' He paused sneakily. 'It gets a little heavy now so no charges, right?'

'Right.'

'Okay. You're a cunt, Mr Ng, but you've always been straight with me. Anyways, Robbie didn't come back with nineteen grand for me. He came back a double murderer, which did me no good at all.'

Ng nodded his sympathy. 'What was Mr George doing in Fasser's dungeon?'

'I was weighing up whether to trade him to the cops for future favours or get Fasser to kill him. It had to be one or the other. Robbie was way out of line.'

Mortaferi moved to the bar and poured himself anothery. Stella's Beefeater was long gone but she didn't ask. The sooner she was out of there, the better. Mortaferi quaffed and waited. A minute rolled by as wheels turned in Ng's head. He stood and didn't offer his hand.

'Thanks.'

'That's it?'

'That's it. May I use your phone?'

'Sure.'

Ng moved to Mortaferi's landline phone as Mortaferi looked pleased and cleansed. Confession, Stella thought, not for the first time in her life, really is good for the soul.

Ng had tensed up. He lowered his voice to a hiss and spoke quickly. He hung up.

'Mr Ng, Miss Pentangeli,' said Doc

'Bye,' said Stella as unshakily as possible, which wasn't very.

*

Instead of asking her to drive him to Best Rest or One Police Towers, the mysterious Ng insisted that Stella drop him off at a nondescript corner in Sweethurst. She waved him goodbye, turned the corner, U-turned and waited. Two minutes later, an unmarked police car pulled up driven by SPC Playne. As they sped off Stella felt a pang of unreasonable jealousy that it was Pauline driving Ng.

26.

death in the dungeon

Stella ate Pauline's dust. Equipped with one of those portable police siren/lights, Pauline's car made Stella's V-dub look like a pile of under-cranked tin. But they were near Wuthering Park. Stella guessed Yasser Faser.

She turned her V-dub into Yasser's street, which was now lit up by half-a-dozen cop cars all with silent sirens and flashing lights. Fasser's house was cordoned off with POLICE: DO NOT CROSS tape. A throng of neighbours behind barricades were looking impatient and bored, as though they'd been there a while and nothing was happening and if something didn't happen soon, they'd be wanting their money back, please.

'Keep moving, m'am. Nothing to see.' A uniform waved Stella on.

Might as well try a bluff, she thought. 'Investigator Ng sent for me. I'm Consultant Pentangeli.'

'Don't care. Keep moving.'

Stella whipped out her notebook. 'Name and badge, sunshine.'

'You call me "sunshine" again and I'll haul in your arse.'

'Name and badge, sunshine. Investigator Ng's gonna wanna know.'

The uniform's eyes clouded over. 'Just a minute.' He spoke into a squawky talkie. Stella heard Ng's garbled voice: 'Let her through.'

The uniform smiled cheesily. 'Park there m'am. Go right in.'

Stella didn't cheese back. 'You deaf? Name and badge.' He gave them to her. She pretended to note them down then parked, figuring, What the hell, the moron will spread the word to tread careful around the bitch in the V-dub. That couldn't hurt.

As she strode toward Fasser's house Stella was favoured with nods and smiles. One cop even lifted the POLICE: DO NOT CROSS tape for ease of passage. Christ! No wonder Ng stayed clear of most cops. Thick as bricks.

Both bodies were on the floor in the dungeon: Yasser Fasser and Nelson J. Sharp, swollen and putrid. Nelson looked like perhaps he'd died easier. His face and neck were pale and bloodless. There was a surgically neat knife gash at his throat. His eyes were half-open and calm. He wore an incongruous smile, as though – just before he died – he'd seen the face of his god YHWH.

Fasser's hands had been duct-taped behind his back and whatever he'd seen at the end wasn't holy. His eyes were open in horror. His clothes were scattered round and he was naked with deep cuts all over his body. Specialists (Coroner's Support) later confirmed his clothes had been removed piece by piece and the cuts made pre-mortem. In his mouth was a blackening bloody package of meat; his penis and testicles had been sliced off and crammed there.

*

It smelt like nothing on earth. The Specialists (Crime Scene and Central Forensics) were at work measuring, photographing and dusting the steel dungeon room. They had bandanas or surgical masks or handkerchiefs round their mouths and noses.

Ng had one hand firmly clasped over the bottom half of his face and was scoping the scene with his MiniCam 3000. Stella, partly to stop herself from screaming, covered her nose and mouth with both hands.

Besides two corpses, there were a dozen lively cops in the house. But except for a soft 'You get that angle?' or 'Over there' or 'Uh huh', the place was as quiet as the dark ocean deep. Ng ran a silent ship. Like a submarine, thought Stella feeling bubbles of panic rising.

*

Ng led Stella outside. 'This is not for you.'

'I'm in this too.'

'This is not for you,' he said again.

She walked off to her car.

*

Ng fussed. Ng barked orders. Ng drove them hard. He made sure each Specialist got everything and a little more. He sent Pauline back and forth to One Police Towers ferrying samples of crusties, latents and cigarette butts. Ng seemed to trust no other cop – from the newest uniform to the oldest hands – except her. He pointed to her police-issued squawky and her private mobile and said, *'Don't use either of them.* No investigation information goes out over any mobile or squawky. Understood?'

'Yessir.'

Even from her car across the road, Stella could read the signs. The cops were grumbling. She could read their minds. 'Ng doesn't trust us? Well fuck him!' Cops slouched a bit more ostentatiously, took their time a bit more exasperatingly. They were finally punishing Ng for years of refusing to play with them.

*

Stella turned on an Angela Drumm CD.

> *How does it feel?*
> *How does it feel?*
> *Love in the air?*
> *Death in the alley?*
>
> *How does it feel?*
> *How does it feel?*
> *Not too scary?*
> *This killer love?*

She felt nothing.

An hour, two hours later, she saw Cordelia Heath step from the gawking crowd to hand Pauline a cardboard tray – a Sweethurst Caff gourmet take-away pack. Pauline and Cordelia's fingers touched during the transfer. Then Stella lost it – crying so loud she had to wind up the windows and turn up the music. In the middle of this horror, someone could still think to bring food and warmth to a lover. *But who will care for me?*

She had just stopped crying when, from nowhere, Cordelia knocked on her window and handed her a second Sweethurst Caff gourmet take-away pack. Cordelia had the sense to keep walking as Stella started howling again.

*

Finally Ng sent the Specialists and uniforms away. Night fell. Ng just sat there alone in some world whose name only he knew.

He didn't sit in the dungeon. That would stink of the dead forever. He sat near the open front door with a view of the living room and the steps leading down to the dungeon where the bodies had been, and looked and remembered this detail he'd noticed and that bit of info he'd gotten from Pauline or some Specialist, uniform or neighbour.

Ng was doing what he did best. Putting two and two together. Then another two, then another. Then subtracting one and moving it nearer the top of the puzzles people in his world called 'events' and 'SODs' and 'doing clients'.

He made a dozen and more calls on a public phone near the corner. Not once, Stella noticed, did he need to use an address book. Stella guessed most of the calls were to Ng's informants or stoolies, or whatever they were called these days.

Finally Ng stood up, nodded goodnight to the uniform watchman and walked over to Stella's car.

'Could we meet tomorrow? Noon? My place?'

'Sure.'

'Thanks.' He looked exhausted. Pauline, dozing in the police unit, would drive him back to One Police Towers where, Stella knew, more and heavier hours awaited him.

27.

balls

Constable Playne was not surprised that Investigator Ng kept mum about her unprofessional behaviour and Cordelia. Not a whisper. His word was always good.

A couple of Specialists (Latent Prints, Body Parts) and one Specialist (DNA, Seeds, Fibres, Assorted) had heard whispers about some love affair Playne was having. Her crush on Ng was common knowledge.

'Ng finally got his leg over Playne. Bet ya.'

'Ng and *Playne?*'

'Hey Pauline, is it true?'

Pauline's first instinct was to deny it. Her second instinct – very Ngian – was to publicly ignore it but privately indicate it was true, thereby deflecting gossip away from her dark mistress.

The day after the discoveries in the Fasser Dungeon, the needling became too much.

'I hear you and Ng are doing it,' said a uniform. Boom! Just like that, SPC Playne flipped and fractured the uniform's nose.

'Paranoid.'

'Mad as a cut snake.'

She was called to Connie's office and fired.

'Specialist Probationary Constable Playne, you are exactly

that – a probationary constable. Pack your shit and get out of
One Police Towers. Bye bye.'

An hour later, Ng burst into Connie's office.

('Like he owned the fucking place.')

He told Connie that if Specialist Probationary Constable
Playne were not rehired in the next five minutes, he would
quit. He threw an affidavit on the Connie's desk. On it were
the names of a six top police – Weismuller, Elmo, Lincoln,
Brix, Greystoke and Ely. If Ng walked, they planned to walk
with him.

'You have thirty minutes to contact Constable Playne and
get her back.'

'Then he walked out, the prick.'

Pauline was rehired before she'd finished cleaning out her
desk. Word spread rapidly and those who liked Ng liked him
more, and even those who didn't like him one little bit liked
his balls.

Connie and a few Deputy Connies saw in Ng's actions the
measure of the police officers they once had been.

28.

who did these four
clients and why?

Room 11 Best Rest Motel. Stella sat primly on Ng's bed.
Pauline sat in the comfy leather like she'd been here before lots
of times, and Stella couldn't help but wonder if they'd ever
done it.

Ng handed her a large gin. 'Oh, it's far too early for me!' she
trilled unconvincingly. Ng put the glass next to her on what
looked like a plywood and cardboard side table. Stella was
impressed that he had bought a bottle of Beefeater gin. To
seduce her? Nah.

Maybe he thought she wouldn't be able to handle Ng's
gruesome MiniCam movie. Well, she'd seen a man crushed,
woken next to a man with a knife sticking in his chest, spied a
man lying scalded and soggy in a shower stall and eyeballed two
stinking bloated corpses. She could handle a movie, thank you.

Pauline, who strangely enough, was casually dressed, was
looking pretty good. Whatever Cordelia had ought to be bottled.

Then it got strange.

Pauline Playne casually lit up a marijuana joint, a veritable
cigar of impressive size, and huffed and puffed on it without a
care in the world. Ng uttered not a word. Jesus! Somehow
Stella had been transported to a parallel Room 11 in another

universe. The No Nonsense Virgin had become a Baby Dyke sucking a spliff in front of her boss who was, in turn, planning to play some après-snuff movies from his own private collection.

Pauline handed Stella the joint and Stella took a hit while Ng, still in his well-cut dark suit, looking for all the world like a headwaiter at some high-class gin and opium den, readied his MiniCam screen.

*

None of Ng's bosses had ever liked Ng's insistence on using his own private equipment for taping crime scenes and formal interviews and informal chats. There were Specialists units for that. Ng's defenders pointed out that the bosses should be happy. Ng was spending his own unpaid overtime looking at crime scenes on his own private equipment. As one Minnie put it: 'That video shit of Ng's solved more events than Agatha Fucking Christie.' The Ng Film and Video Academy was kept open.

*

'Before we start, Miss Pentangeli, everything that happens in this room stays here. It is not for talking about to friends or publishing on your website. Okay?'

'I promise.'

'Constable Playne's drug use is a crime. Your watching these tapes is a crime. My showing you these tapes is a crime. So today we are all criminals.'

Stella nodded, already a bit stoned. She loved it when Ng got all formal. Ah, fuck it! She took a swig of Beefeater.

'This much is plain,' Ng said formally. 'Mr George was in prison during the murders of Clients Sharp and Fasser. If Mr George had a co-conspirator in Bushy Creek, these last two events were committed by this co-conspirator.'

'This co-conspirator must be Superman,' said Stella, 'Fasser was a killer. A mean son of a bitch. He would take quite a bit of killing.'

'Good point.'

'And why Nelson?' Stella was warming up. 'Why kill Nelson? What was Nelson doing at Fasser's anyway?'

Pauline, understandably fixated on a sexual motive: 'Maybe Fasser liked young boys.'

'Don't buy it,' said Stella. 'If Fasser was into young boys, he wouldn't be into a Nelson Sharp. Lost his looks. Too old. Too nuts.'

Ng stopped them. 'Too much speculation. Client Sharp died in the living room, then was dragged down to the dungeon. His neck had been manually broken, not by karate, but rather with a neck-twist — the way gamekeepers kill birds. Client Fasser was done in the dungeon with a large kitchen knife.'

'Like Google.'

'Except Client Fasser was repeatedly stabbed and his testicles and penis had been sliced off and left in his mouth.'

'Smells like sex to me,' said Pauline doggedly. 'Both bodies contained TranQuax in varying degrees. Just like Google.'

'The knife was not found but there's evidence it came from Client Fasser's kitchen,' said Ng. 'The DNA found on the cigarette butts was all Clients Fasser's and Sharp's. The cigarettes themselves were Chesters — the brand Client Fasser always smoked.'

'What's with the dick in the mouth?' asked Stella.

'Shirt-lifting shit-fight,' Pauline responded.

'Maybe Robbie's co-conspirator didn't like gays.'

'Then why not do both?' said Ng. 'Two sets of genitals, two sets of mouths? The co-conspirator had plenty of time.'

'Come on, sir. Let's see the movie,' said Pauline.

'We'll start with the latest event.'

Ng turned on his latest home movie, a travelogue of quality round the killing grounds: Stella's Faust Hall cubicle, Faust Hall's shower block, the Faustian forest, Yasser Fasser's suburban home with built-in dungeon.

*

Fasser's living room is clean but in extreme close-up a large damp stain – not blood – is on the carpet. Water? Gin? Vodka?

Close-up: an ashtray. A dozen or so cigarettes. Same brand. Chesters. Two glasses, almost empty. Water? Gin? Vodka?

The dungeon is horrible. The bloated body of Fasser, genitals in mouth, lies next to bloated Nelson, a bloody towel from Fasser's bathroom next to his body. Extreme close-up of Nelson's neck. Stella takes a huge slug of Beefeater and pours another.

Lots of tiny cutaways of minor details, even a brief snippet of a cheeky uniform poking his tongue out at Ng's camera.

The shower stall at Faust Hall is better. Emu is naked on his belly. The water still running hours later, his skin pruney and scalded. Extreme close-up: bodily waste that somehow hasn't made it down the drain yet. Faeces probably. Close-up: his dead eyes open. He looks disappointed.

Compared to the dungeon and shower stall stuff, the footage of Stella's room is positively genteel. Ng must have been taken it while the Bushy Creek plods were holding her downstairs and the old local doctor was pretending he knew what he was doing. The vision of Lou with a knife in his relatively bloodless chest looks rather tame to Stella by this time. *Maybe the Beefeaters have kicked in.*

Various close-ups and extreme close-ups of bits of Stella's gin stash. *How embarrassing.* Extreme close-up of three used condoms in the wastepaper basket. *Oh Lord!* Extreme close-up: a bottle of TranQuax half-hidden in her suitcase.

The forest outside Faust Hall is a blessed relief. The area where Robbie George lay in wait for two days looks like Little Eden, and in close-up the Bloodspoor's flagons are giant glass houses for orchids.

*

Throughout the whole of 'Who Did These Four Clients And Why?' Ng had inserted cutaways that he thought important. A lot of stuff had been edited. After the first viewing, Ng, Stella and Pauline skipped back and forth and paused and rewound and fastforwarded and reviewed and finally played out whatever joy the movie was going to give them. Brainstorming began.

The Chesters cigarettes were interesting, of course. Fasser had obviously given them to penniless Nelson. A lot of them, Pauline pointed out. He was showing his new boyfriend how generous and caring he was. She was sticking to her rough sex theory.

They all agreed that the doer had left the dead clients in the dungeon hoping they'd stay undiscovered for a month or a year. They agreed also that Fasser's repertoire included great power in his tiny hands. He was the logical suspect to have broken Client Sharp's neck.

'Then again,' said ever-contrary Pauline, 'it could be our missing co-conspirator.'

'In either case, it's not a woman – no offence, ladies,' said Ng. 'I don't mean to insult your gender but a cold-blooded killer with hands strong enough to snap a neck *has* to be a boy.'

Stella burst out into laughter. She wasn't sure he'd been joking but it was as funny as shit.

'What about your mouth, Miss Pentangeli?'

Stella looked up at him in alarm. 'I beg your pardon?'

She flushed. Then Ng flushed and hastily scrambled to make himself plain.

'I meant – during the viewing, did your mouth go dry?'
'Oh.'

Both flushed deeper and the three-second silence seemed forever. This time, Stella scrambled. 'Run the video back to Fasser's lounge room,' she said.

Ng obeyed.

'Something's odd there.'

Ng looked at her eyes. They were glazing over in what he'd come to call her '1,3,2/1,2,3.' look. She'd once told him about Angela Drumm and her song:

> 1, 3, 2.
> 1, 2, 3.
> Sherlock Holmes, man,
> Got nothin on me.

Her '1,3,2 1,2,3.' face was intense. 'There they are! Pause and zoom in,' Stella ordered.

Ng zoomed in and there it was – the reason Stella's mouth kept going dry whenever Ng's MiniCam scoped Fasser's living room.

Books. Stacked in a corner like so much unwanted crap to be picked up by the Good Samaritans, were three books. *Shakespeare's Compleat Works*, Jane Cameron's *Dickens For Juniors* and S. Chrestman's *Long To Reign Over Us – A Brief History of England's Sovereigns*. No cop in this city, let alone Ng, was naïve enough to think that crooks and books don't mix. Years before, one of the state's most homicidal crooks admitted that the reason he'd turned bad and robbed and killed and so forth was to upgrade his private First Editions library. It was considered one of the finest private collections in the world and, when the crook died, a grateful government gladly accepted the 'collection entire' which the doer had willed to 'the people of his nation'.

But in Fasser's home?

Stella spoke for them all. 'Fasser was the kind of guy who, if he found a book, would sniff it in case it was edible and when he found it wasn't, use it for a hammer.'

Ng nodded. 'Yet these books looked like they'd been there in this corner for a while. Why?'

Ng was about to tell Constable Playne to go get the books but she was already climbing into her coat en route to the Police Towers Major Crimes Of Violence evidence lockup.

Ng: 'Don't forget to get receipts.'

'Yessir.' And she was gone to secure the little pile of books, to take them to Ng's office. Stella had spotted what every murder police prays for – a piece of the crime scene jigsaw puzzle that just didn't belong there. Ng was sure of it. The books would lead them to the truth and to the murderers.

29.

la grande étoile

At about the same time as Ng was switching on his home movie, Lucy Sky began strumming at the Sweethurst Caff Back Garden Wednesday Lunchtime Blues and Folk Hootenanny.

> *I know who I am*
> *I know what I is*
> *I'm black and I'm proud*
> *Mind your own biz (ness)*
> *I'm a B.L.A.C.K. man.*
> *Yeah.*
>
> *My mother was black*
> *My daddy was white*
> *He taught me to fear*
> *She taught me to fight.*
> *I'm a B.L.A.C.K. man.*
> *Yeah.*

At the words 'I know who I am', the crowd started to roar and applaud and whistle and stomp. Lucy had to strum empty time until they calmed down enough for her to continue the song.

It had become dead Emu Gentle's anthem. Tears flowed with the beer and Lucy was made to sing 'Black Man' over again.

Which pissed off the lyricist Cordelia Heath a whole lot, although she was showbiz pro enough to smile every time the little slut shook her arse and sang her crappy tune.

*

Cordelia and Milton Shaver, a large round face on top of a larger round body with round hands clutching a round cigar, sat at a table at the back of the green and tended Back Garden of the Caff.

Milton was 60 but looked 40. He'd known a few – not many – clients to whom fame had come late-ish and they were the tough ones. They were tigers who prowled their turf and ate their young and spat at intruders with ears flattened back to protect their fame. They knew it was a chancy thing. Young folks who get success early on can be careless with it – they reckon there's plenty more where that came from.

Except there isn't.

Milton had seen young 'uns rise and fall in the blink of an eye, in the space of a tantrum, in an argument over who had the biggest trailer on the film set. Then he'd seen them crumble slowly from the inside as they realised that it . . .

wasn't coming back.

They'd been let in the front door via the red carpet and they were thrown out the back into the stinky alley, their foreheads marked 'Never To Be Readmitted To The House Of Repute'. Sad. Pitiful. While they were his clients – his family – Milton cared and worried. When he cut them loose or vice versa, he couldn't give a shit. Fuck 'em. They blew it. Beat it.

'She's got no right to sing the song, Milton,' said Cordelia. 'It's mine!'

'Listen to 'em. The crowd loves it. They love her.'

177

'But it's not the melody I wrote!'

'Where is the melody you wrote?'

'I didn't write a melody. I'm not a composer!'

'So she's written a melody. What's the prob?'

'The problem is she's stolen my melody.'

'But you ain't got a melody!'

'That's not the point!'

'The crowd loves the words. They love the tune. They love the whole fucking song. So what's the prob?'

But Milton knew the prob. It was the prob every goddamn client he'd ever massaged and groomed and made millions for had. The prob was that this cute young broad with the voice of black soulster was pulling the focus away from Cordelia Heath and Cordelia Heath's play and all things Cordelian. Milton puffed on the round cigar and blew round rings into the night air. 'Let me give you a word of advice. I know songs. She can write the tunes. Let's include her in.'

'Include her in what?'

'In the whole thing. The play. The movie. Let her do the tunes. Great tits. Can she act?'

Milton hid his amusement at the rage flooding into Cordelia. Partly he was messing with her. He didn't give a shit who wrote the songs. He didn't give a shit if the cute little broad on stage played the black guy's wife or not. He was here for the deals. He was — in spite of his cruel mind-messing — here to advance the best interest of Cordelia Heath, his newest family member. He loved her. After all, 25 per cent of the pot at the end of this murder rainbow was worth a lot of love.

*

Lucy could feel Cordelia's fury from the stage. She could also feel the approval of the fat guy sitting next to Cordelia. Older men always dug her.

Smiling to their table, Lucy launched into the song she knew would stiffen the sinews of Fatso over there next to Cordelia. The Fortnight crowd had loved it. Fatso would cream his pants.

Pull up the shade
let some light in the room
open the window too.

Shake up the mattress
straighten the bed.
It's over.

Make me some tea
drink it down slow
pretend I'm drinking for two.

Shower real slow
let the water flow.
It's over.

He wasn't much of a man
but he was alright
He made me comfortable
ev'ry night.

He wasn't much of a man
but he was okay.
I wish he was with me
today.

Oh yeah, the Big Man was lapping it – and her – up. She felt consumed by a fire inside, as if her talent were doubling by the minute. She was taking dictation from Zeus.

179

*

The rage she felt when she found Cordelia wasn't home scared Pauline. Was she at the Lady Love bar? No. The Sweethurst Caff Hootenanny? No. Finished.

Quick call to Police Towers Ops. Unofficial all points. Bingo. Cordelia's crappy car parked outside the Étoile.

And now here was the night clerk, smiling and impressed by her ID, telling her that yes, Mr Shaver and a guest had arrived, oh an hour ago. Female. 30ish. Blonde. Striking looking. Suite 1001.

Oh God! Her angel! With Shaver? With that fat cunt! Her rational mind was telling her, 'Calm down! Of course she's with the fat prick. He's her agent. He's trying to make her rich!' but, of course, not only didn't she listen to her rational mind, she put her mind on her growing list of enemies.

Night Clerk, Cordelia, Shaver, Mind. She was giving wet head to the pig. After all, that's what Pauline used to do in high school to any boys who asked her out. Night Clerk, Cordelia, Shaver, Mind, Boys, Men, Past, Present, Future. The Hate List kept growing.

She could kill.

Oh yeah! she could kill all right. Him first, then her.

She tried the door to suite 1001.

It opened and there they were — Shaver on a stuffed couch, Cordelia standing at the window and big-titted Lucy sitting cross-legged on the floor, white panties flashing, strumming her fucking guitar and singing one of her fucking songs, her mouth frozen open mid-warble. They all looked at her in freeze frame, the very picture of innocence and music with not a naked bit anywhere.

Pauline felt herself shrinking back into the No Nonsense Virgin of yore. With the look of contempt Cordelia was giving her, there was no doubt it was all over forever and ever between them.

'Just what do you think you're doing?' said Cordelia.

'I thought you and . . .' her right arm waved at Milton but she couldn't finish the sentence.

'What? You thought I was having sex with *him*? And this . . . this child too? Is that what you thought?'

'Poopsie, I'm so sorry.' Pauline's voice was a strangled whisper.

'I've had it with you. I wouldn't take abuse from Robbie and I won't take stalking from you.'

'Please.'

'Get out.'

'Cordelia.'

'Any stuff you've got at my place, move it out now, tonight, or you'll find it on the street tomorrow.'

Grotesquely, Pauline tried to hug Cordelia, to pull her back to her, but Cordelia slapped her arms away. She saw nothing in Cordelia's eyes. No love. No hope. Nada.

30.

ties that bind

Tout le Sweethurst knew Cordelia Heath had taken up with an SPC Playne who followed Cordelia round like a puppy dog and knew nothing about anything except, apparently, dead bodies and blood stains. Big surprise – Cordelia had finally dumped her. Now Heath was humping that fat bastard from LA to keep him sweet so he'd make her rich and famous.

'This Shaver guy's so twisted he makes Cordelia do . . .'

'He's evil! He hypnotises babes and . . .'

'He makes that young chick singer Lucy *watch* while he and Cordelia . . .'

Who wouldn't weep? Pauline had learnt an invaluable lesson about showbiz and life. Rumours are always true. Even if they're not.

*

Ng pushed at the door to Pauline's tiny flat. It wasn't locked, and opened with a horror-movie creak.

He and Stella entered to find the flat was filthy. Cartons of grief abounded. Chocolate biscuits, chocolate ice cream, chocolate milk with peanut butter like mother used to make.

Pauline emerged from the bedroom dressed in a ratty woofy

tracksuit with chocolate stains all over. 'Oh God! I want her back!'

Ng let her take his hand and lead him to her messy kitchen table where, in an island of clean, lay the two letters her poopsie had sent her when they were lovers.

'Listen, sir. Listen.'

Pauline picked up the first letter, written on the back of a Faust Hall menu, and read it aloud. 'Dear one. I don't really know who you are but can we meet later tonight? In your room? To talk? Cordelia Heath. PS Please. Please.' Pauline's eyes said it all. We met. We were shameless.

Then she read the second letter, her dreamy smile saying, This one's even better. 'Darling one. Meet me at Lady Love. 8. Don't be late. And keep your eyes off any strange women until then. God! You're so wonderful. C.'

Pauline beamed madly at her boss through her tears. 'I was her darling. I was wonderful.'

Some instinct – maybe her mouth was dry – told Stella to look at the letters. She took them gently from Pauline's hand.

Deer One. I don't realy know who you are but can we meat later tonight? In youre room? To talk? Cordelia Heath. PS Please. Please. Please.

Darlling one, meat me at Lady Love. 8. Dont be latte. And keep youre eyes of any strange women until then. God! Your so young! So wonderfull! C.

Cordelia, so tall, so blonde, so Viking, so tough, wrote like a seven year old – like this: *Deer Penttangeli Papers The jokes on you! I put them both to sleep then kiled them. Googel was a Jew. Gentel was a shitskin. Thus all members of the white Race will aveange.*

Ng locked eyes with Stella, and knew immediately that

she was in Sherlock Holmes land, putting pieces together. 1, 3, 2. 1, 2, 3.

*

Milton Shaver had prepared for an unpleasant afternoon with Cordelia Heath.

Like every Hollywood heavy he knew and had ever known, Milton refused to read anything longer or more complex than a racing guide or an obit column. Reading was what 'they' did. The minions. The worker bees. Milton's best worker bee was Andreea Maddox, a black chick straight outta Compton, LA. They'd grown old together, her with her nose for story and characters and the right ingredients for the right decade, he with his packaging and chutzpah and bullshit. Shaver and Maddox. Lou and Andreea. Salt 'n Peppa.

Every year, Andreea threatened to leave him. She was 62 now and rich. She didn't need this tinsel shit any more, she'd tell him. Every year he upped her salary, bonused her blind, begged her to stay just one more year – and every year she allowed herself to be stroked and paid for and needed. After all, as Milton had long long ago figured out: 'What's the point of life in LALA – shit, of life *itself* – unless you're in showbiz?'

All Milton knew about 'Midwinter dead black dreams' or 'Midwinter black nada nada' was that he hated the title. The rest Andreea could tell him. In short sentences with short words in them. And she'd told him that morning – night time in LA.

'You're *paying* for this shit?' Her voice came through loud and clear on the Swan-shaped telephone. 'It's crap.'

'How come?'

'You ever heard of William Shakespeare?'

'Sure. Plays for the Red Sox.'

'Charles Dickens?'

'The Yankees? Short stop.'

'Ho fucking ho.'

'Andreea, Andreea, Andreea – do you kiss your mother with that mouth?'

'I read it twice. The second time to see if you were joking. Dreams of a dead *black man*? Uh huhn. No way. Sorry. This is lots of bits of dreams of dead white men. All stolen.'

'Run that by me again.'

'Okay. Listen. The very first scene. Did you read it?'

'No.'

'Did you look at it?'

'No.'

'Jesus Christ. What do you *do*?'

'I pay you.'

'It goes like this. Benjamin Franco – he's the black guy, the hero, the dead guy that has all these crappy midwinter dreams. With me so far?'

'I guess.'

'Okay. He says this.' Her voices changed from her usual Transatlantic Educated to homeboy. '"She talking to me. Angel. You're like what they call a comet. You're a messenger and I'm a-lookin' at ya in the lazy clouds."'

'He says *that*?'

'Page one.'

'What's it mean?'

'"She speaks/O, speak again, bright angel! for thou art/As glorious to this night, being o'er my head/As is a winged messenger of heaven/Unto the white-upturned wondering eyes/Of mortals that fall back to gaze on him/When he bestrides the lazy-pacing clouds."'

'That's even worse.'

'That's Shakespeare, you idiot! This Heath woman's obviously just grabbed any bit of Shakespeare she came across, messed around with it and put in on the page.'

185

'Oh.'

'Quote unquote – "Mary: Alas my love you'd do me wrong if you throw me away. Ben: Yeah dat'd be rude. Mary: I've been in love with you so very very long. Ben: Me too. I loves your company." She's not even trying now. That's "Greensleeves".'

'"Greensleeves"?'

'The song "Alas, my love" – even you must know it.'

'Oh. Right. I heard that. Is it copyright?'

'Jesus, Milton! Henry the Eighth wrote it over four hundred years ago.'

'So it's outta copyright.'

Patient silence. Then Andreea: 'This is my favourite: "Ben takes a gun from the desk drawer, puts it to his head. Ben: I can't live this way no more. Mary, I'm coming home."'

'What's that from? The Torah?'

'"Barney Miller".'

'"Barney Miller"?'

'The cop show. Word for word.'

'"Barney Miller"?'

'Milton, I had a guy run data checks on all the shows playing there during the last six months. In Ep 119 Detective Fish stops an old homeless man from shooting himself after he's stolen Barney's gun. Fish wrestles him to the ground. But just before he does the homeless guy says . . .'

'Lemmee guess – "I can't live this way no more. Mary, I'm coming home."'

'You got it.'

Andreea heard Milton's mind turning from across the waves. She knew plagiarism per se wouldn't bother him. Outright theft per se wouldn't bother him either – Milton, Hollywood, LA, the world were built on it. But Milton would absolutely *hate* paying good money for stolen goods he could get for nothing. And, much as he loved lying to people, he couldn't abide being lied to. Especially by a broad. Andreea knew this Heath woman was toast — yesterday's toast, chewed by the dog.

Eventually, Milton: 'So. Any *good* news?'

'Some of the lyrics are good. Standard twelve-bar blues, most of 'em — keep that composer you found and at least you got some *great* tunes. Have fun, y'all.'

*

Milton decided to arrange one of his famous French Humiliation Farces, with Lucy in the room playing her tunes and Cordelia outside but not being allowed in until the tension was unbearable. It worked perfectly.

Scene 1. Lucy — clutching her guitar, newly coifed (short, spiky) and confident (black mini) after her first taste of small-time fame — arrives first. 'What did your assistant in LA say about the tunes I wrote?'

'Don't be so impatient. Sing me one of your songs. Not from "Midnight dreams in winter", from before.' Ring, ring. 'Yeah? Send her up. Lucy! Sing!'

Lucy starts:

> *Dear God give me your thunder*
> *Dear Lord please come and help me.*
>
> *I only do your bidding*
> *Please don't stay so quiet.*
>
> *God give me your blessing.*
> *Give me some sure sign.*
> *That what I do is holy.*
> *You must know the answer.*

Scene 2. Knock, knock. Cordelia enters. Imposing, straight, a righteous genius about to have her genius rammed up her arse.

'What did your assistant say? About the play?'

'Shh! Don't be so impatient. Lucy's singing a song about God. Go on chickie-babe.'

> *God now we are partners.*
> *Look how much I've loved you.*

'What did your assistant say?'

'Siddownandshutup!'

> *Lord ain't that something?*
> *Lord ain't that something?*

Scene 3. See, what a thirst for fame does to a proud spirit. See proud Cordelia get them drinks. See Cordelia sit patiently as Lucy sings another song, then another. This French Humiliation Farce is going real good and Milton is loving it until . . .

CRASH! He falls to the floor then . . .

BASH! Lucy's guitar drops from her numb hands and CRASH! she follows it to the carpet.

Scene 4. Milton wakes up handcuffed naked to the Le Roi-size four-poster bed. Next to him, sleeping and fully clothed – damnit! – is Lucy, bound with the sash of his white XXOS towelling robe.

Milton counts himself the luckiest guy in the world. In what other universe would a fat old fart like him – brother of a rabbi, born to be a minor criminal – get all this kinky shiksa gash? Four, five decades of El Primo Off The Hoof pussy. God, he loved showbiz.

Bondage! He's packing wood like he's 16 again. Who would have thought she'd take rejection so good?

Milton finally figures out that Cordelia Mickey Finn-ed him and the Sky chick. Used to be 'ludes. Now it's Tranquil or TranQuax or some shit. Young chick tied to the bed. Old man tied to the bed. Ageing but good-looking broad talking nasty – and this broad knows her nasty.

WHACK!

'Excellent!'

WHACK!

'Okay, already, stop with the—'

WHACK!

'No, no. I'm not in the mood no more.'

WHACK! 'What did your assistant say about my play, Milton?' Her voice low and surreally calm.

Milton's survival instincts take over. 'She fucking loved it, baby. Great play. Better movie. You're gonna make us both rich!'

'Liar!'

WHACK! Jesus – this gash is off with the pixies is what she is.

'I'm telling the truth. Take these cuffs off, lemmee get dressed, we'll make a killing. A fortune, I mean.'

'She hated it, didn't she?' Loud now, then soft – an excellent thing in woman. 'She hated it. Andreea hated the play.' Milton glances down at his groin. Oh woodie! where are you now? Pink, white and helpless he looks up at the woman tall, strong and Viking.

This Cordelia Heath is mad. She is what's-her-name? – the chick in Hamlet who loses it and kills herself. Except this crazy bitch is gonna kill everyone. Oy.

'Okay, okay. Andrea thinks you may have ... erm, taken little bits from other folks. Like Charles Dickson and so forth.' Cordelia is looking away in the distance. Maybe at some spaceship from the Milky Way. Oh Jesus! I'm a goner.

189

Then the Viking woman starts a monologue which includes, it seems, every person she's ever known and every actor or actress who has made more than ten cents a year and every slut or faggot or bitch or wimp or motherfucker who's done her wrong. Mainly, though, she rants about one guy who done her wrong.

'I took you out of prison! I fed and clothed you, Robbie! I made you a star! And you threw it away! And you hit me! You made a fool of me! *You hurt me, you arsehole!* You broke my arm! You broke my heart!'

Louder, baby, louder. Let the staff hear.

'I even gave you another chance! I put you in Fasser's dungeon. I gave you a real prison again. So you could write another masterpiece! For *me*! For *you*! For *us*!'

Milton's brain races. Now I get it. She locked this Robbie guy up and made him write this play!

Cordelia is running hot now. 'Two pages a day! That's all you had to do. One month! A new play by Robbie George!'

A new thought takes her over. 'Except why should you be the star? I did all the work! Why not me for a change?'

Milton figures there are a lot more than just three people in this room.

Then Lucy stirs, 'Hmmm' – until nestling child-like against his shoulder she wakes with an –

'*Ahhh!*'

That's it, Lucy, scream honey. Maybe Crazy Gal here will do you first. Your death screams will bring someone running to my rescue. If he was Cordelia, he'd shut Lucy up first and right now.

Lucy screams more. That's it. Scream those gorgeous lungs right out!

Cordelia picks up an ice pick from the bar. Lucy shuts up. Viking woman grabs Lucy by the chin and moves in so their faces almost touched. Her voice goes creepy soft and low. 'I can

stab you or I can bash your empty little head on the floor. Who
you do you want to be, bitch — Lou? Emu? Nelson? You can't
be Yasser because I've saved that role for Milton.'

Milton, ever the producer, can't help himself. 'Which one's
Yasser?'

'The Arab! I cut off his dirty prick and his dirty balls and
stuffed them in his dirty mouth.'

Oh. 'And you want me to be him?'

'No. I don't want you to be *him*. I want you to be *dead*.
I want you to be dead with your *dirty prick* and *your dirty balls
in your dirty mouth*.'

Milton feels his wise old cock shrivel into his body. Then the
door opens quick as death and — like a weird mirage — a tiny Jap
guy is pointing a gun at the crazy bitch. Suddenly she's all over
the Jap, bashing and flailing, and even though he could stop her
with his gun, he wimps out. Now she's biting him in the neck
like some vampire and gets a grip on his nuts right through his
suit pants and is twisting, twisting, twisting them like plums
on a tree all the time wrestling for the gun. She gets it and the
Jap's doomed and so are they all when some white-haired
woman rushes in and screams '*Noooo!*' and jumps on Fruit
Loops who seems to have ten arms and kicks the woman . . .

CRACK! CRACK!

Two shots in rapid succession and blood cascades out of Viking
gal's lovely twisted-in-pain mouth, but she's still wriggling . . .

CRACK! CRACK!

At the door stands a second skinny mottled-from-crying
woman with a service revolver. The crazy Viking eyes go dead
and she falls straight-legged and face first onto the lush carpet.
BLOP!

Milton starts to faint but Lucy's screams startle him awake.

epilogue

NG TRIUMPHS!

SHOWBIZ P.I. A LUCKY LADY

THE DETECTIVE AND THE DAME

'An insoluble SOD and Ng made it look like child's play.'

'What if that Cordelia bitch had done Milton Shaver? A Hollywood Player! This town would never have lived it down!'

'Investigator Ng's future with the police service has never been stronger or . . .'

*

Stella and Ng mopped up the rest of case quickly.

There was no 'second co-conspirator'. Fasser had been more than willing to follow Cordelia's order to break Nelson's neck in the dungeon — only to fall under the weight of Cordelia's TranQuax and wake up dead with his dick in his mouth.

Doc Mortaferi had told Ng one teensy lie. It hadn't been Robbie George who'd gone to Mortaferi with the plan to get his 19 grand back. It was Cordelia. Mortaferi got off scot-free — which, for this city, was about normal.

*

'Why did Cordelia kill Google?' Even as Stella asked, she knew she knew and she answered herself. 'She wanted a nice juicy scandal to advertise "Midwinter dreams". Lou Google's blood was publicity to her. The more blood the better.'

Neither of them brought up the logical extension of this which was – Stella's blood would have been even better PR. *Did Cordelia choose Lou instead of me by eenie meenie minie mo?*

Further. 'There's no way to prove it,' said Ng, 'but I suspect Ms Heath killed Client Gentle for only one reason: he didn't like the play.'

'*That* I can understand.'

Ng looked at Stella to see if she was serious but Stella had her Ng face on.

'Ng, who was it shooting those bullets through Mortaferi's windows?'

'Off the record?'

'Sure.'

'My previous superior, Hawkeye. Until he lost his eye, he was a marksman for Specialists (Special Tactics and Response). I promised I'd get him his job back if he did a favour.'

'You can get him his job back?'

Ng pondered. 'Today I can. Next week – who knows? Sometimes they make me play politics.' A new thought. 'You were never at risk in Mortaferi's house, by the way,' Ng continued. 'I told Hawkeye if you were in the slightest danger, he was to shoot all of them.'

It was Stella's turn to look at Ng to see if he was serious. For once, she could read him just fine. He was as serious as death.

*

193

Milton Shaver signed Lucy Sky to a five-album deal. Her first magnificent effort – the soundtrack of 'Midwinter Dreams' –

got four and a half stars in *Rolling Stone*. She moved to Beverley Hills.

*

Of the other Fortnight players, Jeddah Magnum also came out the most okay. Cordelia's instincts about publicity for 'Midwinter dreams of a dead black man' and The Fortnight turned out to be accurate. Now that the killer was safely identified (and dead), bookings for the next year started to flood in. Jeddah moved out of the trailer park and into a Bushy Creek townhouse more in keeping with her status as head of one of the world's leading playwright conferences.

*

A rumour — barely a whisper — started floating round the corridors of power that Stella Pentangeli had documentary evidence linking Hawkeye to an 'assault and intimidation by fire-arms incident' involving a well-known citizen. Further whispers suggested the evidence would go away if Hawkeye was reinstated. Minnie and Connie — in fact the whole political/policio establishment — knew it was Ng pulling the strings but they could neither prove it nor resist it. Hawkeye got his job back.

*

Only Terry Dear's singular and insular life was unaffected by the 'Murders at The Fortnight'. 'One of the joys of a dedicated cyberlife,' he said to Stella over coffee at the Caff. 'The real world's just a stage. I just watch.'

194

*

Stella and Ng went to see Robbie George in prison together. He was up on some half-arsed charges that he was a co-conspirator in four deaths – or maybe five if you counted Cordelia. 15 to life. Ng had no doubt his – Ng's – current juice could make it all go away but Robbie stopped him. Robbie had had enough enough enough of life on the outside. Inside he could function. Inside he could breathe. Inside he could write. Ng and Stella finally convinced him that 15 to life was too long and Ng arranged for him to cop to 'reckless indifference' with a max of two years. Robbie went along with it but fooled them all by pretending to try to stab a screw on his second week in. He got 15 to life.

He had an idea for a new play.

'What's it about?' said Stella.

'It's about love and fame and how it all starts dying as soon as it's born. Maybe I'll set it at a playwrights' conference.'

*

SHOWBIZ! SHOWBIZ! SHOWBIZ! ONLINE!
THE PENTANGELI PAPERS *EXCLUSIVE*

It all really started five years ago when they let Robbie George out of prison. The sun was coming up, the tiny side gates opened and there he was. He looked great, like he'd been doing push-ups or jogging or whatever they do in stir for exercise. The officers made jokes . . .

Also by Wakefield Press

The Analyst

Fred Guilhaus

Henry Sinclair is attracting a celebrity following for his newspaper columns about money and love. He has observed that in this anxious world, partner choices seem to be made just like share purchases.

A group of social climbers has adopted him – but each for a self-serving reason. With his best friend, Alex, and his girlfriend, Rosie, Henry becomes enmeshed in their alien world of luxury yachts and parties.

As the bank forecloses on his parents' cottage and 'the group' unravels in its own deceit, Henry must make his choices. For all his business knowledge, he has never played the market to his own advantage. Now, perhaps, he needs to serve two masters.

For more information visit www.wakefieldpress.com.au

Also by Wakefield Press

Lady Luck

Kirsty Brooks

Introducing Phoebe Banks, the luckiest lady in crime . . .

Phoebe is freshly dumped, like an old Pepsi can on the side of the road, by a boy with bad hair riding a Ducati. Lumping her earthly possessions, along with the limp scrap of dignity she has left, she hitches into Adelaide and arrives hot, tired and desperate for a Snickers bar. So she isn't exactly jazzed to discover her ex-boyfriend was also a drug-dealer, and she's accidentally ended up with his merchandise.

And then she meets Sebastian. He's probably the best catch in town until she discovers he's got a past as dark as a new pair of Docs. But Phoebe's no stranger to underworld characters and she figures she might as well take advantage of her situation, as young people are encouraged to do in the free-market economy. It's about then that Jackson Sinclair, the impossibly sexy policeman, starts asking some difficult questions and Phoebe has to figure out if she wants him to kiss her or cuff her.

Lady Luck races along on a sassy ride of love, disaster and junk food as Phoebe tries to get her life back together, dodge some of her dubious new acquaintances, and maybe get laid. Although a really good snog would probably do in a pinch!

For more information visit www.wakefieldpress.com.au

Also by Wakefield Press

The Trojan Dog

Dorothy Johnston

'I should ask your department's accountant whether he's missing nine hundred thousand bucks.' This is the anonymous message that will change Sandra Mahoney's life.

When a powerful but unpopular bureaucrat is accused of theft and computer fraud, Sandra is convinced that the charge is false. But how to track down the culprit when almost anyone could be an enemy? In her search for the truth, Sandra finds herself in a battle of wits against an elusive and unscrupulous opponent, a battle in which no-one's allegiance can be taken for granted.

The Trojan Dog is a compelling story of computer crime, loyalty and betrayal against the backdrop of a city – and a country – on the cusp of political change.

For more information visit www.wakefieldpress.com.au

Also by Wakefield Press

The White Tower

Dorothy Johnston

'Jumpers,' McCallum was saying. 'Jumpers are – well, in my experience jumpers are always badly disturbed. They choose to jump because it's so violent.'

A mild young man's addiction to a role-playing internet game has led to his death. Disturbingly,his suicide is a bizarre echo of his chilling execution in the game; his only note a digital mirror image of his own death.

   But where do blame and responsibility lie, in a world where powerful men are as seductive as they are unscrupulous? Sandra Mahoney finds that the threads of truth and illusion can easily wind into a choking scarf of manipulation and deceit.

For more information visit www.wakefieldpress.com.au

Wakefield Press is an independent publishing and
distribution company based in Adelaide, South Australia.
We love good stories and publish beautiful books.
To see our full range of titles, please visit our website at
www.wakefieldpress.com.au.

Wakefield Press thanks Fox Creek Wines
and Arts South Australia for their support.